Whatever it Takes

BRENDAN MAGUIRE

Cover design by Gillian Baines (Fiverr)

Table of Contents

Acknowledgements

This is my opportunity to say my personal thank you to a few important people who have helped me along my writing journey.

To my wife Gill, for her forbearance, patience and unstinting moral support during the last few months when I have been somewhat absorbed in my crime novel.

To the invaluable help in proof-reading provided by my daughter Laura, my sister Joan, Julia Weedon, Jane Connor and Fiona Henderson. Also, my thanks go to Eric Gartrell and Hayley Walsh for providing me with an insight into police workings within England.

Finally, a special mention to my editor-in-chief, the ever-attentive Gillian Baines for her invaluable support and dedication to the task.

My heartfelt thanks to you all.

Dedication

To my three children, Barry, Laura and AJ who
make me feel one very proud father.

Prologue

Thus far, it has been a pretty ordinary, balmy August day. I have been working hard alongside my mum and dad in our corner general store in Westwood, a leafy suburb of West London. As constant trickles of perspiration run down my back, I fleetingly feel slightly envious of my younger sister, Aasha, who has opted instead for a career in medicine and is currently studying at King's College. An image flashes through my mind of her sitting in the sunshine enjoying a drink with friends outside the university union.

It is now approaching early evening, customer numbers are beginning to dwindle and my mum is grasping the opportunity to leave a little early in order to go home to cook dinner. In a light-hearted manner, she warns my dad. 'Darling, I am going to prepare your favourite this evening, so don't dare be late.' Sadly, this is one meal my dad is never going to live to enjoy.

I, too, choose to leave a little early as there is a long, chilled pint of lager in a frosted glass with my name on it in our local bar. Leaving my dad to deal with any stragglers and to close up for the evening, I slip away while the going is good. In retrospect, this decision is to represent a very poignant sliding doors or if only moment in all our lives.

My dad, Harinder Singh, also known as Harry, has owned and run this business for some twenty-five years. Admittedly, my viewpoint could be perceived as being just a tad subjective, but he is truly a gem. He is held up as a pillar of the local community and is loved and respected by young and old in equal dollops. He is also a prominent member of the local business owners' council, which greatly enhances his profile. In truth, he is pretty much an institution within the Westwood area.

And behind every good man, there is a good woman. My mum, Meeta, is renowned for carrying out various charity funding projects in the local community and is equally popular with all our loyal customers.

Oh and by the way, my name is Charanjeet, known by friends and customers alike as Chas.

Chapter 1

Derek and Olivia are in their mid-forties and have been married for twenty-one years, and for a couple of them – the first two – Olivia could perhaps, just perhaps, lay claim to having been relatively happy. She cannot say that she was not warned. Quite the contrary as she can vividly recall being lectured to by her parents regarding the dangers of marrying Derek quite so soon after meeting him.

'Olivia, you hardly know him or his family.'

'You would perhaps be better to wait for a year or so.'

'You don't know enough about him yet.'

'It could be the biggest mistake of your life, Olivia.' And other such equally prophetic remarks.

In retrospect, I suppose Olivia had only known Derek for about three months when they were wed. It was love at first sight, although as it transpired, sadly not of the everlasting variety. At the time, it appeared that Derek had all the credentials a girl could possibly desire. He was tall, dark, handsome in a rugged kind of way and extremely attentive. Having piercing dark brown eyes and an innate charm, he also possessed a keen sense of humour. Furthermore, he had a real presence whenever entering a room. Looking back, Olivia was the object of his charm offensive and she fell for it hook, line and sinker.

It was generally accepted that among her friends, Olivia was the good-looking one in the group, and perhaps not without foundation. With a flawless complexion, Olivia was tall, blonde, with an eye-catching figure, penetrating almond-shaped eyes and a beguiling smile. Despite her appearance, she often portrayed a hard side to her personality and she made it abundantly clear that she was not one to be messed with.

Clearly, having now the benefit of hindsight, perhaps Derek simply wanted someone pretty on his arm in the hope of further enhancing his street cred. However, once they were married, all seemed to change. Moreover, once she became pregnant, his attitude deteriorated even further. Perhaps having a pregnant wife by his side was not quite the image he had wished to convey. From then on, their relationship went steadily downhill. Sadly, with every passing month and year, Derek seems to have shown less and less interest in his wife.

Maybe she could have coped with the lack of attention and simply embraced her grandiose lifestyle; however, she has other genuine causes for concern. Of late, Derek has been becoming more and more secretive about his business. On the face of it, he owns and runs a property development company which is proving to be ultra-successful if the trappings are any indication. Nevertheless, why all the covert meetings? Why always leaving the room to take phone calls? While Olivia has heard murmurings of affairs, she knows this is something different, something equally secretive. Also, some of the characters he has been inviting into their house have been particularly shifty in appearance.

'What was that meeting about?' she would ask and would be greeted with a typically patronising response: 'Don't you be worrying your pretty little head, darling, just leave me to look after the pennies,' or some other such equally dismissive retort. To be honest, it has now reached the stage whereby Olivia opts not to enquire any further and simply concentrates all her efforts on helping Derek divest of his substantial and very possibly ill-gotten gains.

Whoever first said that money can't buy you love had it spot on. Yet, to the outsider, Olivia appears to have it all. She has not worked since she was married. She has a very handsome - if not adoring - husband, a shiny new convertible sports car sitting in their triple garage and all the time in the world to pamper and indulge herself. What's not to like?

Her two closest friends, Constance and Felicity – known as Connie and Fliss – are quite incapable of disguising the fact that they are very envious of her lifestyle. To be honest, Olivia would be lying if she did not admit to occasionally revelling in watching them turn green before her very eyes. Having said that, they and their respective partners would still be considered to be well off, but of course everything is relative in life.

Connie is very tall in a willowy type of way, extremely trim and undeniably flat-chested. She is so skinny, she most likely has to jump about in the shower to get herself wet. She has very distinctive looks, having short blonde hair cut in such a neat bob that at the front it borders on being pelmet-like. One of her many attractions is her truly infectious laugh which on occasion resembles more of a trademark guffaw. Connie is the manager of the local Westwood Estate Agency which greatly enhances her capacity as a purveyor of local gossip. It is quite amazing the insights she has into her clients' lives when she is selling their houses – perhaps second only to being a personal hairdresser or personal trainer. She is married to Nigel who owns a very small car showroom specialising in prestige motors. One has the impression that if just one car a week were to depart his forecourt, it might be cause for a mini-celebration.

By contrast, Felicity, although of wealthy stock, constantly bemoans the fact that she has married below her station. Her husband, David, is a civil servant and is as handsome as he is boring and predictable. He is totally devoid of charisma. Looking positively, she need never worry about security as David will absolutely ensure that their finances are kept in check and there are no unnecessary extravagances. Before David came on to the scene, she enjoyed suitors aplenty. Felicity is dark-haired, petite, dimpled and cute in a koala kind of way. She has not worked for many a year, although if pressed on the subject, she would say that she is involved in the cottage industry. Whenever the notion takes her, she dabbles in creating greeting cards. She claims that it provides her with that little bit of independence, not to mention some handy pin-money.

Derek and Olivia were blessed with two children – well, adults now, really. Perhaps someone should have invented a word for grown-up children as they, with some justification, dislike being referred to as 'kids' or 'children'. Anyway, they have Mel, aged twenty-one, and Miles, aged nineteen. Derek seems to feel that throwing money at them is the universal panacea and also his own personal way of expressing love. Olivia's view: 'If only he were so giving of his time.'

Mel has been a model child and has never given them any cause for concern. She is currently working as a hairdresser, and it is Derek's intention to buy a salon for her once she has a little more experience under her belt. She also has a steady boyfriend, Stuart, who seems a decent sort of a guy and who is very loving towards her. Derek and Olivia are both firmly of the view that they will be married before too long, have children and ultimately live happily ever after.

By contrast, Miles has always been a bit of a loose cannon, particularly in his teenage years. From a very young age, he was always getting himself into bother of one kind or another. Although he has never had any brush with the police, he has come fairly close. He was bright enough but never showed any real commitment at school, and this was reflected in his results. When it came to him leaving school, Derek was of the view that his best interests would be served by joining his property development business. He said that he could then 'keep a close eye on him'. Sadly however, this move merely exacerbated the problem as he then very quickly became too big for his boots. The situation worsened as Derek continued to spoil him. As soon as he turned eighteen, his father bestowed on him a brand new, brightly coloured BMW sports car coupled with a cherished, private registration number plate and his own personal expenses account. Whenever challenged by Olivia as to whether this was a good idea at his relatively tender age, Derek's response was always a fairly standard one.

'At least that will stop him drinking if he has to drive home after a night out.'

In retrospect, perhaps it might not be drink that could be his undoing – rather something a little stronger.

It is true to say that Miles has always been the 'golden boy' as far as his dad is concerned, and very sadly, he has only ever paid a passing interest in Mel. When Olivia gave birth to Mel, Derek simply could not hide his disappointment at her not managing to immediately provide him with a male heir to carry on the family name. Suffice to say, he was then doing metaphorical somersaults when Miles came along and has continued to spoil him ever since. In Derek's eyes, Miles can do no wrong. How misguided can one man be?

Chapter 2

'Right, ladies, here's to a good night out,' says Felicity as she raises her glass of champagne and clinks glasses with her girlie pals, Constance and Olivia.

'Cheers' they all announce in unison.

They are attending a local fashion show sponsored by Derek's property company, DL Developments, as clearly evidenced by the blatant if not somewhat crude signage adorning the premises. Not surprisingly they have ringside or 'catwalk-side' seats. They are being treated like royalty, a testament to the high level of sponsorship provided by Derek Lamont. Given Derek's non-attendance, it is abundantly clear to all that Olivia is thoroughly enjoying being queen bee for the evening.

They are all suitably dressed for the occasion. None more so than Olivia, whose extremely fair skin is allegedly a legacy from her Danish grandmother on her mother's side. Olivia has never been a shrinking violet and has opted for an off-the-shoulder, backless, fuchsia pink dress with a neckline so plunging that she could be in danger of being arrested for indecent exposure. To add to the ensemble, she is wearing killer heels.

By contrast, Felicity is sporting a bright and cheery, black and white polka dot top which immediately brings Dalmatians to mind. This is complemented by a leather miniskirt clinging to her like shrink-wrap. Felicity has also put her hair up on this occasion, thereby reducing slightly the height difference between herself and their hostess for the evening.

From bitter experience, both girls know better than to attempt to outshine Olivia at the risk of not being invited to any future events. To be candid, their relationship with Olivia is somewhat superficial, albeit mutually beneficial. Constance and Felicity are generally available to attend many opulent events such as this one, with the added perk of VIP treatment. In return, they not only serve as Olivia's mini-entourage, they also make her look good. Adhering to this theory, Constance has opted for a relatively mundane blue trouser suit with a pair of silver sling-back shoes.

The champagne continues to flow in direct proportion to the casting aside of inhibitions and the wagging of tongues. As is par for the course, Olivia begins to bemoan her lot and is clearly not full of the joys. In essence, Derek is not showing her sufficient attention. All the while, the other girls are thinking that they would gladly walk in her shoes – even for just one day. Then again, I suppose the other grass is always greener.

For the umpteenth time, Olivia leaves the table to mingle with those more worthy while Constance and Felicity admire the clothes being modelled, catch up on a little girlie gossip and imbibe bubbly.

'Fliss, I wonder how many of these models Derek has bedded?'

'You are naughty,' Felicity responds. 'I suppose he must be getting some bang for his buck,' she adds.

Her unintended innuendo prompts one of Constance's trademark guffaws which comes to an abrupt and unnatural end as a swirl of fuchsia approaches.

As the evening wears on, the ever-constant topping up of their champagne flutes is definitely beginning to take its toll, especially on Olivia. She is becoming particularly animated and is very noticeably slurring her words. In an unsubtle attempt to show that she is in need of a champagne refill, she balances her fluted glass on her head and then laughs hysterically, her rising shoulders causing it to ultimately fall off and smash into smithereens. This serves as an opportunity for Constance to indulge in even more guffawing.

Then, as if a cloud has appeared over her head, Olivia suddenly becomes very sombre, almost morose. It is no surprise to her friends that her next topic is the state of her marriage to Derek – and they are not disappointed.

'I never should have married him, you know. I should have listened to my parents. He treats me like dirt and keeps so much from me. So, I don't feel guilty spending his money. If I tell you girls something, will you keep it to yourselves?'

It is evidence enough that she has over-indulged if she imagines that they are not likely to repeat it. They both nod in agreement, but not too enthusiastically, lest she changes her mind.

'I suspect Derek might be dealing in drugs.'

They both feign complete surprise, whilst at the same time express concern for her situation. Constance leans forward in a sympathetic manner and suggests that she should confront Derek in the hope of clearing the air.

'I have attempted to raise the subject with him,' she says, 'but on each occasion, he has just become angry and bad-tempered.'

'Has he ever been violent towards you?' asks Constance.

'Not physically, but he has been very threatening towards me.'

At this point, Olivia resorts to tears before clicking her fingers to order even more bubbly. The evening then degenerates into somewhat of an alcoholic blur.

Chapter 3

Johnny Morgan is having a quiet night in the house when his mobile rings.

'Hi Johnny, Miles here, how's things? Fancy hanging out for a while this evening?'

Johnny has no plans but is a little reluctant to accept. The reason being that a week or so earlier, they teamed up together and it was a bit of a disaster. In fact, Miles was almost in danger of being arrested. He had been high on a cocktail of drink and drugs and was caught dealing drugs whilst they were in a nightclub. He was forcibly removed and on leaving the club took a wide swing at the doorman causing him bodily harm. The club owner and the doorman decided not to take the matter further, but Miles was barred from future entry to the club.

Miles and Johnny had been in the same year at school and had been close buddies since first year. In modern parlance, I suppose they would be described as being 'besties'. However, since leaving school they have, to a certain extent, drifted apart. Yet this has been more by accident than design. The major contributory factor is that while Miles has joined his Dad's property business, Johnny has opted for a degree in business studies at a local university. As a result, while

Miles tends to have free time each evening, by contrast, Johnny is much more likely to be found on campus attempting to catch up on his studies. In addition, a considerable financial gulf has arisen between them. To Miles, money is now never an issue. In fact, he could be accused of being too keen to 'flash the cash'. By comparison, Johnny does his level best to survive on a meagre student loan topped up by some much-needed cash earned as a DJ at the occasional event. As a result of this imbalance, he is sometimes made to feel awkward, particularly if it is Miles's turn to buy a round when he often opts for a bottle of champagne. He seems oblivious to the fact that this causes others, like Johnny, a certain degree of embarrassment.

In the last couple of years, Johnny has noticed a major change in Miles – in his behaviour. He used to be such an easy-going, fun-loving guy with no real agenda. Now however, whenever they are out and about, he is a completely different animal. He possesses an air of superiority – a polite way of saying he is 'up himself'. This appears to derive from driving a flashy car and his seemingly unlimited cash resources, courtesy of Bank of Dad. Also, after a few drinks, he now has a tendency to seek out trouble.

Shortly before 7.00 pm, his bright yellow BMW sports car pulls up outside Johnny's parents' house, a blasting horn announcing his arrival. Before Johnny reaches the front door, it sounds again and again. Upon opening the passenger door, Johnny is greeted by strong and pungent alcohol fumes. The little angel on his right shoulder tells him not to get into the car whilst the little devil on his left shoulder is virtually holding the door open for him. He stands hesitating for a moment before the devil wins the day – a decision he will sadly regret for many a long time to come.

Johnny has no sooner entered the car when it becomes abundantly clear to him that Miles is completely high. He suspects that this is on a concoction of drink and drugs. He takes off at considerable speed, and at one point, the car even mounts a footpath. Johnny's heart is in his mouth while his stomach is doing somersaults. He yells at Miles to slow down. His protestations fall upon deaf ears as Miles steers the car with one hand and drinks from a can of beer with the other. Each uttering from Johnny results simply in the music being put up a further notch as 'Bat out of Hell' by Meatloaf fills the evening Westwood skies.

Johnny is mightily relieved when he eventually slows down and comes to a halt. As Miles reaches for the handbrake, Johnny grabs the can of beer from him and throws it out of the car window in the interests of self-preservation. But his relief is to be very short-lived. The car has come to a stop outside Harry's local corner store.

'No probs, plenty more where that came from,' Miles proudly announces – or words to that effect. Johnny immediately senses an opportunity to escape, even if it entails a rather long trek home. He decides that he will wait until Miles is inside the shop and then seize the moment. Such procrastination he would also live to regret.

Miles approaches the shop like a centipede with ninety-eight missing legs. At the same time, Harry, the proprietor, is exiting the premises and is literally turning the key in the front door lock.

'Harry, open up. I want a few cans of beer.'

'Sorry, I am closed now.'

'Well, you can bloody well open up then.'

'Sorry Miles, but I'm already late for my dinner, and anyway, I don't like your attitude. You have obviously been drinking and should not be driving.'

'Like I fucking care about your dinner or whether you like my attitude. You lot would not have food on your table if it were not for the likes of us giving you business. Just open up the fucking shop and get me some beers pronto, you bastard.'

'Miles, I have to close sometime and Meeta will have my dinner on the table. I am not re-opening the shop – end of story.'

At that point, Miles blocks his passage, taking a menacing stance. Then it all kicks off in a flash as Harry tries to usher him out of his way by gently steering Miles to the side.

'You fucking bastard, who do you think you are raising your hand to me?'

Miles is immediately enraged – a man possessed. Quick as a flash, he strikes Harry with a ferocious right hook followed by a rapid couple of blows to his stomach. As Harry doubles up racked with pain, Miles takes a couple of steps back and then kicks him on the head with extreme force as if attempting to kick a football from one end of a football pitch to the other. Harry collapses in a heap in the doorway. The gut-wrenching sound of his head striking the tarmac will live with Johnny for evermore.

Johnny is frozen to the passenger seat as this attack is taking place. It will be to his eternal regret that he did not intervene, although having said that, it was all over in the blink of an eye. Panic sets in and Johnny flees the scene on foot. His lasting image is of Miles standing over Harry and an ever-increasing pool of blood forming on the pavement. This image keeps playing within his head as if on a loop. Somewhat eerily throughout this fleeting attack, Johnny could hear the constant ringing of a mobile. He later discovers that this call was from Harry's wife, wondering why he has not yet arrived home for his evening meal.

Johnny considers phoning an ambulance, but then his phone might be traced and it might be alleged that he is in some way involved in the attack. Why are there hardly any public phones in the area? He convinces himself that someone will have come across Harry pretty quickly and will have called for assistance.

He runs and runs until he can run no further. His clothes are saturated in sweat and he feels sick as he is still unable to remove the mental image of the ferocious attack from his mind. His phone rings. It is Miles. He ignores it. It continues to ring and ring. He is not for giving up. As Johnny sits on a garden wall trying to regain his breath, he eventually elects to answer one of his many calls. At first, all he can hear is constant sobbing on the other side of the phone. Perhaps naively, he initially assumes these are tears of remorse – sadly not.

'Johnny, what have I done? I don't know what came over me, but Harry should not have started to get physical with me. You must surely agree. Please tell me that you won't mention what happened to anyone. We have been friends for a very long time. I promise I will give up taking drugs. Please, please Johnny. My whole life could be ruined.' This is then followed by more inconsolable sobbing.

'Have you phoned an ambulance?' asks Johnny.

'No,' he meekly responds.

'Well, I believe there are still one or two public phones at the train station. Go there and phone for an ambulance urgently.'

'Okay,› Miles responds, wishing to desperately interpret this suggestion as an indication of some kind of collusion on the part of Johnny. At this point, Johnny cuts the call and continues on his way home.

Chapter 4

As suggested by Johnny, Miles makes his way to the station, driving as quickly as possible but, at the same time, not wishing to attract the interest of any passing police patrol car. He has to constantly wipe tears from his eyes whilst digesting the reality and magnitude of what has just happened.

If only … that bastard Harry had opened up the shop when I asked him to. If only Harry had not pushed me. After all, he started it. If he had not laid hands on me first, none of this would have happened. Yes, it is really all his fault. Obviously I am entitled to protect myself. Anyone else would have done the same in this situation – surely? He had just about managed to convince himself.

Having arrived at the train station, the realisation strikes him that his shirt is covered in Harry's blood. Thankfully he has a casual jacket lying on the back seat of his car which he quickly zips up to his neck before entering the train station.

He dials 999.

'Hello?! Help!' Miles says breathlessly.

'…And what service do you require?' comes the voice at the other end.

'Ambulance, you need to get an ambulance.'

'...What is the nature of the injury?'

'A man's bleeding very badly.' More breathlessness.

'...What is the location?'

'Outside Harry's Corner Store in Bridge Street, Westwood.'

'...And who is calling?'

'Just go, quickly.' And then the receiver is replaced, with Miles feeling very marginally better about himself.

Miles then drives home but with a detour via Bridge Street. Ironically, he recalls reading that it is very common for an offender to return to the scene of his crime. He cannot understand why he has chosen to do so – there is no rationale for it. As he gets closer, he is met with the screeching sound of a siren as an ambulance passes him by. He approaches the scene from the other side of the road and spots two police cars parked outside Harry's store, and they have already cordoned off the area by means of red tape. He drives past at a steady pace, again not wishing to attract any interest.

He says to himself that there is no way that they will be able to connect him to the assault; after all, there was nobody else on the street and he did not leave any calling cards. Now homeward bound, he checks in his interior mirror that there is no evidence of him having been crying. He also keeps his jacket on when entering the house and makes a mental note to wash his shirt at the first available opportunity.

His dad calls to him from the lounge when he hears the front door opening. 'Is that you, Miles?'

'Yes, Dad,' he responds from the hallway.

Miles feels it will only arouse suspicion if he retires to bed without speaking to him face to face. So he stands at the lounge door while his dad sits back on the couch nursing a large glass of red wine.

'You're home very early!'

'Yeah, I'm not feeling great.'

'What's wrong with you, son? I hope you'll be okay for work tomorrow as it is going to be a busy day'.

'I'll be fine, I will just have picked up a bug. I'll have an early night and should be right as rain in the morning.'

'You look troubled. Also, why are you wearing a jacket when it is so hot?'

'Maybe I have got a temperature,' he lies.

'You haven't bashed your car, have you?'

'No Dad.'

'Good night, son, sleep well.'

'Good night, Dad,' he says, knowing full well that no amount of counting sheep will allow him to enjoy his slumbers.

Chapter 5

It is the morning after the night before in the Lamont household. Derek, Mel and Olivia are sitting around the breakfast table as Miles comes down to join them. He looks absolutely shattered and is clearly not in the mood for any casual chit-chat.

'Your dad said you were not feeling too well last night and you came home early. How are you feeling this morning?'

'I'm fine, thanks. I think I am on the mend,' replies Miles, somewhat unconvincingly. He is so conscious of his parents watching him while he is eating breakfast that even if he had nothing to feel guilty about, he would probably look guilty.

The local radio blares out the Bob Marley classic, 'Three Little Birds'. "Don't worry, about a thing, 'cause every little thing, gonna be all right."

Olivia's maternal instincts somehow suggest the sentiments expressed in the song are not mirrored in the Lamont household on this particular morning.

The seven-thirty morning news then comes on. 'A man is in hospital in a critical condition having been seriously assaulted in Bridge Street, Westwood yesterday evening. The police are appealing for any witnesses to come forward.'

Miles is unsure if anyone else is listening to the news report – fortunately it seems not. Upon hearing it, he has to run to the toilet to be physically sick. Olivia feels quite unnerved as her maternal instincts tell her there is obviously something troubling Miles, and her concern is that he has been still been dabbling in drugs. Upon his return to the table, his mum lectures him on the dangers of drug-taking. However, there is little point in pursuing this in front of his father as it would simply be met with 'boys will be boys' or some such other standard response. Heaven forbid that his darling son might have acted inappropriately.

Interestingly, 'Goody Two-Shoes' Mel sits there, not uttering a word, probably preparing to polish her halo.

Chapter 6

Detective Inspector Jean Ronald is with the major investigation team (MIT), part of the Homicide and Major Crime Command, based at Scotland Yard.

She could be fairly described as being a career woman. From a very tender age, she had wanted to join the police and she ultimately fulfilled her ambition. She was particularly thrilled when she was promoted to Detective Inspector.

Aged in her mid-thirties, DI Ronald is also single. Having said that, those who know her well would be inclined to say that she is married – but to her job. In any event, given the strength of her current commitment to her work, there would barely be sufficient hours left in her day to facilitate the kindling of any semi-permanent romantic relationships. Nevertheless, she has had a few dalliances, but whenever there's been a choice between romance and her work, there is only ever going to be one winner. She had been engaged to one of her suitors, but it only lasted about three months as it became clear to him that there would be three of them in any ensuing marriage.

Stoic, resolute, determined and ambitious would justly describe her characteristics. While not perhaps the warmest person upon first meeting, she is however very much respected by peers, adversaries and subordinates alike. If she were to be likened to an animal, then a bulldog comes to mind; certainly not in terms of looks but in terms of her stubbornness, determination and never-say-die attitude to solving cases. If the detective constables who report into her had to choose an epitaph for her tombstone, it would probably be 'hard but fair'. Yes, the force has high hopes for this rising star.

Any limited spare time she does have tends to be spent with her parents. Her father contracted Alzheimer's at a relatively young age and her mum has been his carer for the last few years. So Jean Ronald will regularly spend time with her dad in order to provide her mum with some respite. It really saddens her to see her dad's health steadily deteriorate. He has a combination of good days and bad days. In the case of the latter, there are some occasions when he struggles to recognise her, which can prove to be extremely distressing. Jean and her mum have tacitly accepted that once the deterioration has reached a certain level, he will ultimately have to go into a care home. However, they will stave off that day for as long as possible. Jean will probably admit that one of the attractions of absorbing herself in her work is that it serves as a welcome distraction from dwelling on the inevitability of her dad's condition.

DI Jean Ronald has had the unenviable task of calling to visit Meeta Singh and her two offspring who were all understandably completely distraught and shell-shocked.

'Please do rack your brain and let me know if there is anyone at all you can think of who might wish to harm your husband?'

'Honestly, I have tried and absolutely nobody comes to mind. He is a loving, kind and caring person who is liked by friends, family and customers. He does not have a bad bone in his body,' Meeta replied.

'Do you have any CCTV showing the outside of your premises?'

'No, only inside as we never considered it necessary. We have never had any problems in the past.'

'Ok, I will arrange a car for the three of you to go to hospital to see him. However, please be aware that he is still unconscious. And please brace yourselves as he does have substantial facial injuries. Finally, please be assured that I will not rest easy until I have apprehended and charged the callous individual or individuals who carried out this vicious and cowardly crime.'

Chapter 7

It is the morning after the assault and DI Jean Ronald is standing adjacent to the ubiquitous whiteboard. She feels completely drained and lacking in energy. During the previous night, she received a call from her mum to the effect that her dad had got out of bed and was hallucinating, believing that someone was breaking into their house. She went over for two or three hours until her dad had calmed down and her mum's fear had abated.

DI Ronald has already attached to the whiteboard photos of the victim, his wife and two children with names below each one for identification purposes. Called to this briefing are Detective Constable Janet Green and Detective Constable Andrew Gordon. While both DCs are a little wet behind the ears in terms of actual experience in their current roles, what they lack in that department they more than make up for in enthusiasm for the cause. In DI Ronald's world, the latter carries far more weight.

DC Andrew Gordon is a relatively late recruit to the police force, having joined only three years ago about the time of his thirtieth birthday. Although he has always been single, he has had no shortage of admirers and a fair few girlfriends over the years. DC Gordon is bright enough but never applied himself in his school days. While a number of his classmates went on to further education, he did not have the necessary qualifications and opted instead for a sales position in a local furniture shop. In the short-term, he was the winner as he was earning hard cash, but as the years passed, most of his friends overtook him in terms of earning capacity. DC Gordon was however a real asset to the company, and his gift of the gab served him well, especially since his position was partly commission based. Before too long, he was promoted to assistant manager, a position he occupied for a few years. Nevertheless, he did not feel fulfilled. One of his friends had joined the police force, really enjoyed it and influenced DC Gordon to apply. The rest is history.

In her mid-twenties, DC Janet Green is a credit both to herself and her police force. Her greatest assets being her boundless enthusiasm and natural zest for all aspects of life. Unlike her immediate boss, DC Green has a perfect work-life balance. Having said that, she still has strong ambitions as far as progressing in the police force is concerned. She and her live-in partner, Alice, have been together for almost three years and are currently talking about tying the knot.

DC Green and DC Gordon also make a good working team; there is definitely mutual respect there, and on a day-to-day basis, they get on together extremely well. However, they both require rhinoceros skin as verbals are being regularly batted back and forward.

'Right, let's get started!' says DI Ronald. 'Last night at approximately seven p.m., the victim, Harinder Singh, known to all as Harry, was viciously attacked outside his corner store in Bridge Street. It apparently occurred as he was closing up the shop at the end of his working day. He is currently in Moorfield Hospital in an extremely serious, probably critical condition. It is already abundantly clear that he is a particularly popular and respected figure in the community. I would go as far as to say that it appears he is a bit of a local treasure. For this reason and given his ethnicity, this case is likely to have a relatively high profile. We are going to be very much in the spotlight, so let's make one enormous effort to catch the perpetrator as soon as possible.

'Harinder is married to Meeta Singh and they have two adult children named Aasha and Charanjeet, known to friends and customers alike as Chas. Charanjeet works in the family business, while Aasha is currently studying medicine at university. Let me say at this stage that there is absolutely no suggestion or indication whatsoever that the family are in any way involved in this assault. This is not a line of inquiry we will be actively pursuing, although as always, no avenue is ever completely closed to limits.

'Given that Harinder and his family do not appear to have any known enemies, we should be alert to the possibility that the attacker may well be from outside the immediate area. Equally, we should not entirely be ruling out the possibility that the attack may have been racially motivated.

'Andrew, I would like you to check any neighbouring commercial premises as well as all residences in the close vicinity to see if there is any CCTV which covers the entrance to the corner store where the attack took place. I can confirm that the Singhs do not have any external security cameras in situ. Please check through the tapes of the internal CCTV and highlight anything to me that seems out of the ordinary.

'We have already carried out an initial examination of the locus. Please check if anything of evidential value has been turned up. In particular, please consult with forensics. Also, following our press release, I have set up a special incident direct call line.

'Janet, I would like you to speak to the emergency services. The initial information received is that there were two emergency calls made by two separate individuals. Please interview them both. We will resume with a follow-up meeting at 08.30 tomorrow. Thanks for your time, and let us hope that very soon we will have a name in the frame for this heinous crime.'

Chapter 8

For Miles, every minute and every hour is dragging by as slowly as a snail at a snail funeral. He feels sick to the pit of his stomach. In one crazy moment, he may have ruined his whole life, not to mention having risked the possibility of having to do lengthy jail time. He has tried to phone Johnny on numerous occasions, but he is once again blanking his calls, and it seems he wants nothing more to do with him. It is imperative that Miles knows what Johnny is going to say if he is ever interviewed by the police.

What if he decided to tell all to the police? What if someone else actually did witness the assault? What if the incident has been caught on CCTV? What if ... what if...?

Miles has just made a personal promise to his maker that he will never again touch drugs if he will only make this matter go away. All the while, he is wishing he had found more time for religion in his past. What he would give to just have some normality back in his life.

Just as his mood is spiralling downwards at a great rate of knots, a call comes in for him. He glances at his mobile and is greatly relieved to find it is from Johnny. There is a God!

'Hi Johnny', he says in an attempt to sound casual, if not upbeat.

'Have you been listening to the news?' Johnny asks.

'No,' Miles replies, hanging on to his every word.

'Harry is dead!'

Strangely, the words do not fully sink in immediately for Miles as he is in such a state of shock. There is a brief hiatus before he drops the phone and runs to the toilet to be sick. He feels like the bottom has dropped out of his world as he lies on the cold bathroom floor tiles whilst hanging on to the toilet pedestal. Quite apt, he thinks to himself as his whole life is also seemingly going down the pan. The reality hits him. He is a murderer. He could be jailed for years on end.

'Oh fuck!' he shouts at the top of his voice.

#

Meeta, Aasha and Charanjeet had all been present when Harinder slipped away. Sadly, he never did recover consciousness. Harinder and Meeta had been married for twenty-nine years and had already made plans to celebrate their pearl wedding anniversary. After Harinder's passing, the three family members sat around his bed for a couple of hours before very reluctantly leaving his side.

Meeta can simply not take it in. The suddenness of it is just too much for her to handle – one minute he was alive and healthy and the next he had disappeared from her life forever. In almost thirty years, they had not spent one single night apart – they were quite inseparable. She keeps wondering how anyone could have viciously attacked her husband – a man more sinned against than sinning. But quite staggeringly she does not actually bear malice towards the perpetrator of this heinous crime. On the contrary, she merely feels pity for the individual responsible –whoever that may be.

By stark comparison, Charanjeet is consumed with bitterness towards the, to the extent that he almost welcomes some kind of vengeance. But then again, Charanjeet perpetrator has been suffering internal turmoil. Turning over and over in his mind like a tumble dryer is the thought that had he not selfishly left work early to go for a beer on the evening in question, his dad would still be alive. He continually tortures himself with this recurring thought.

As for Aasha, she has simply retreated into her shell. Everyone deals with grief in their own particular way. She has always been her dad's little girl and they shared a special bond – a bond that was very prematurely and very unfairly broken.

Chapter 9

'Good morning,' says DI Ronald to her detective constables. 'I hope you are well rested and are ready to rise to whatever challenges today might bring. As you are now both aware, Harinder Singh has very sadly passed away in hospital and we now have a murder case on our watch. The heat is most definitely on. We owe it to his family and to the public at large to find the callous individual or individuals who carried out this brutal crime. Janet, what have you got to report'?

'Well, Ma'am, the first person who made a call into the emergency services was a Michael Watson, an elderly gentleman who resides on his own just a couple of blocks away from the scene of the crime. He was out for an evening stroll when he encountered the victim who was known to him. While Harinder Singh was still alive when Michael Watson came across him, he was unconscious and remained so. He said that he immediately phoned the emergency services requesting assistance from both police and ambulance services and both arrived within five to ten minutes. He remained with Harry until the services arrived, and a full statement was taken from him at that stage. The victim never did recover consciousness. My view is that Mr Watson will prove to be a very straightforward and credible witness.' DC Green continued. 'The second call was registered a few minutes later and is of more interest as, somewhat strangely, the caller left no name. Equally strange was that the call came from a public phone box, and I am currently awaiting more specifics.'

'Thanks Janet, please keep me up to speed. Andrew, anything positive to report?'

'Not so much, Ma'am. I have canvassed the local businesses, almost all of which were closed at the time of the attack, and so far I have not managed to procure any CCTV which is of any assistance to us. Equally, I have interviewed the majority of local home owners, but that well is also dry. Some of the neighbours were not at home when I called by, and so I will be trying to contact them again today. Finally, I have been in touch with forensics and am awaiting their report.'

'Thanks Andrew, keep on top of the situation. Time is of the essence.'

Chapter 10

There is a strange atmosphere in the Lamont household. In particular, Mel's little brother has been acting very remote and distant and behaving as if he has the worries of the world on his shoulders. In the normal course of events, he is usually in Mel's face – and annoyingly so. He is also spending an unnatural amount of time on his own in his bedroom – hardly healthy for a nineteen-year-old. Her mum has asked Mel to have a word with him. She knocks on his bedroom door and is met with a grunt.

'What do you want?'

'It's Mel, may I come in?'

'Ok,' he replies, somewhat unenthusiastically.

Miles is lying on his bed and has obviously been crying. As siblings, they used to be particularly close when they were younger. However, they have noticeably drifted apart in recent years. This is partly due to Miles's universally obnoxious behaviour in his late teens and partly due to Mel spending so much time with her boyfriend, Stuart. It has not helped that Miles and Stuart have never really seen eye to eye, the latter viewing the former as being immature and a bit of a chancer. Having said that, Stuart is certainly a little older and also more discerning. Nevertheless, the bottom line is that blood is thicker than water and deep down, Mel does of course care about Miles. Whatever happens, he will always be her little brother.

'What's up, Miles, there's clearly something troubling you. Do you want to share? Is there something I can do to help?' This is met with silence. 'Come on, Miles, you are so obviously not yourself at the moment.' Mel can sense he is weighing up whether or not to confide in her and feels she simply has to be a fraction more persuasive or patient.

'There is nothing you can do for me,' he replies hesitantly, but unconvincingly.'

'Try me. Even if I am unable to assist, you know the old saying, a problem shared...' Mel responds while Miles bursts into tears.

'Honestly, it's worse than anything you could ever imagine,' he answers. 'Ok, if I tell you, you must promise faithfully that you will not mention to a living soul, especially Mum and Dad.'

Mel agrees unconditionally.

Miles then proceeds to talk Mel through events on the night in question. Starting with his drink and drugs excess, picking up Johnny, stopping off at Harry's corner shop, then the assault and his hasty retreat. He then speaks of phoning the police before driving once more past the scene of the crime.

Nothing can prepare Mel for what she has just heard. At first, she is completely speechless. In addition, the situation seems so much more real to her as she had personal knowledge of the victim.

'You have to tell Mum and Dad,' says Mel, trying to gather her thoughts together. 'They will know exactly what to do for the best.'

'No way,' Miles responds angrily. 'And remember, you gave me your word.'

Mel's hands are tied and she feels as powerless as a turtle on its back. In the interests of siblings' honour, she will keep her word. She will not even mention it to her boyfriend, but it's not going to be easy.

Chapter 11

'Good morning.'

'Good morning, Ma'am,' the DCs respond in unison.

'And what do we have to report this morning?'

DC Janet Green is the first to respond. 'You may recall the second person who called the emergency services appeared to want to protect their identity. It transpires that the call came from a public phone within Westwood train station. Here is a transcript of the call.'

DI Ronald takes the transcript and studies it:

Hello! Help! (breathless)

...And what service do you require?

Ambulance, you need to get an ambulance.

...What is the nature of the injury?

A man's bleeding very badly. (breathless)

...What is the location?

Outside Harry's Corner Store in Bridge Street, Westwood

...And who is calling?

Just go quickly.

(And then the receiver is put down.)

'Ma'am, there are no cameras in the station which incorporate the area where the public phone is located, but I have been religiously trawling through CCTV coverage of those arriving and departing the train station at the relevant time.' It is a truly monotonous task but DC Green has been, if nothing else, extremely painstaking. She is also very ambitious and so keen to make a good impression on her Detective Inspector.

'Initially, I was scrutinising the footage to identify all those parties who had entered Westwood station any time after seven p.m. and left shortly afterwards. This may sound fairly straightforward as the majority would be entering the station to catch a train and therefore would not be likely to re-appear into view for a few hours. However, there are countless other legitimate reasons why one would enter a station for a relatively short time, over and above making a phone call. One could be visiting a shop, meeting someone off a train, buying a ticket for future travel or simply taking a shortcut by leaving via another exit.'

Before DC Green had become cross-eyed while trawling through the footage, she had chosen to solely concentrate on those people who accessed the station at the entry point nearest to the public call box and who were in the station for a maximum of ten minutes. This narrowed down the field considerably as she now only had about a dozen known runners. Of that number, one young man was of particular interest for two reasons. Firstly, despite the exceptionally warm and humid conditions that evening, he had a thick padded jacket on zipped right up to his neck – somewhat unusual. Secondly, his body language was quite irrational. He was so blatantly harassed and ill-at-ease.

'So, Ma'am, I think I might just have made some progress. Having sifted through the footage, this one person is of particular interest.'

'Very well done. I will have a look at the CCTV footage.' These words are greeted with a self-satisfied, albeit slightly self-indulgent smile.

DC Gordon has nothing else to add, simply saying that there are only a handful of neighbouring proprietors still to be contacted, but thus far, there have been no witnesses. Also, he is still actively chasing up the forensics department.

Chapter 12

Suffice to say, the Singh family are truly devastated and completely grief-stricken. It is bad enough losing a loved one, but infinitely worse when it is so sudden and unexpected. Sadly, their problems do not stop there. A Sikh funeral usually takes place within two to three days of a death. Even this courtesy is being denied of the Singh family because the body of Harinder Singh is having to undergo a post-mortem due to the circumstances surrounding his death. This will inevitably take quite a number of days.

Out of respect, the corner shop is remaining closed for at least one week and Aasha is taking leave from university. Aasha and Meeta have been virtually inseparable since Harry's death. They were close beforehand, but their profound grief has resulted in this bond growing even stronger.

By contrast, Chas has not yet been truly able to grieve. Rather, since his dad's death, he has been undergoing a period of total resentment and anger. Resentment at being denied his father far too young and anger towards the person, or people, who committed the callous and cowardly crime. Chas is truly embittered and strangely has also distanced himself a little from his remaining family.

When the shop is to re-open, it will not be a straightforward exercise from a practical point of view. It will be a gargantuan task to first of all remove the massive avalanche of flowers, wreaths and sympathy cards that presently adorn the shop entrance – a true indictment of the outpouring of love and affection for Harry. Shop customers have also started fundraising to assist Harry's family. In addition, respects are being paid to Harinder Singh at Ealing Gurdwara London Sikh Centre, a place of learning and worship where the Sikh community gathers.

Chapter 13

Having perused the CCTV footage, DI Jean Ronald shares the view that the person identified is at least well worthy of further consideration. At the very least, he is someone that they would want to be able to eliminate from their enquiries.

'Ok, while the image is rather grainy, someone out there will recognise this young man. Please release a still shot on social media inviting the general public to come forward with suggestions as to his identity. If that should fail, then I will seek permission from upstairs to splash out on a statement on primetime TV. Andrew, anything to report?'

'Yes, Ma'am. We received an interesting call on the incident line. A certain Hannah Wilson, a widow in her late sixties, called in to say that she was driving past Harry's shop on the evening in question on her way to meet a friend for a night out. Her account ties in with our own timelines. When driving past the corner store in Bridge Street, she first of all noticed a somewhat flashy, distinctive yellow sports car with a private registration. Then her attention was drawn to an older Asian man and a white youth in his late teens apparently involved in an argument at the entrance to the shop. She only witnessed verbals, no violence. She is of the view that she could most probably recognise the aggressor, if required.'

'Well done to you both. I feel we are now making genuine progress.'

Later that morning, the still photo of the young man in question is aired on social media and the phones start to ring with a fair degree of regularity. One name features far more than any others – that of Miles Lamont.

Chapter 14

Johnny's computer screen displays a photo of his long-term friend. He is fairly easily recognisable as being Miles Lamont, the person the police are wishing to interview. A cold chill runs through his body. In truth, he feels somewhat guilty thinking almost entirely of his own plight, when that of Miles is infinitely more serious.

A multiplicity of questions are swirling around in his head, given that it is only a matter of time before the police spotlight will be focused on Miles, and then perhaps him.

Will Miles mention that I was there? Could I have been spotted that fateful evening? Could I be charged with being complicit in the crime? Should I go to the police to provide a statement? Should I contact Miles and ask him not to mention that I was present? If I say I witnessed the crime, could I be charged with being an accomplice? Oh so many unanswered questions!

Unsurprisingly, Johnny is struggling to keep up to date with his university studies. He simply cannot concentrate, and studying is quite the last thing on his mind at the moment. He keeps trying to rationalise his position.

After all, it is not as if I am a getaway driver in a heist. In any event, how could I have been expected to predict that there was going to be a confrontation, never mind any violence?

Chapter 15

Miles is feeling sick to the pit of his stomach. He is sweating profusely and has a throbbing headache. He is slowly losing the will to live. Mobile phones in the Lamont household are red hot, following the release of the police statement. One minute his mother is yelling blasphemies at him, the next there are eerie silences during which one could hear a pin drop. He does not quite know which is worse. Miles has never heard his mother swear so much.

'You fucking idiot, after every-fucking-thing we have done for you and you bring fucking shame upon your fucking family. How could you be so fucking stupid?'

It seemed to Miles that his mum is more concerned about the adverse effect on her family image than the fact that her son may perhaps have to endure a lengthy jail sentence. In the meantime, Mel sits in silence. To her eternal credit, she acts just as surprised as her parents upon hearing of the developments.

By contrast, Derek is far more pragmatic about the situation. He calmly asks Miles to explain exactly how the assault – or murder – came about.

'Well, I stopped at Harry's to buy a few beers. He was closing up at the time and refused to serve me. Obviously I was a little disappointed if not annoyed. This resulted in an exchange of words, and then out of the blue, he struck me. I struck him back by way of self-defence and I think he must have hit his head off the pavement. I obviously did not intend to kill him, I was just protecting myself.'

'Ok,' says his dad. 'We probably have very little time before the police come knocking at our door. Almost certainly you will be taken down to the police station, so you'd be as well getting yourself mentally and physically prepared for that.'

Almost immediately, Derek is on the phone to Walter Bryson, one of the leading and most expensive criminal lawyers in the country. He is one who 'enjoys' a reputation for sailing fairly close to the wind and, on occasions, also being too close to some of his clients. It strikes Miles as somewhat strange that they are on first-name terms. Every picture tells a story, he thinks to himself. It becomes clear from listening to just one side of the conversation that Bryson is going to be on standby in the likely event of Miles being apprehended or charged. In the meantime, Derek has warned his son not to utter a single word to the police.

Reality strikes home again very soon when the doorbell rings. How ironic that a simple and cheery sounding 'ding-dong' can herald such utter devastation in one's life. Miles is struggling to breathe. His mum looks out the window and upon spotting the police car becomes quite hysterical, crying and wailing. Derek tries to calm her down while en route to the door to usher in the awaiting officers, DI Ronald and DC Gordon. They quickly identify themselves before inviting Miles to accompany them to the local police station to assist with their inquiries. Derek tells the officers that Miles will not be answering any of their questions, and if he is going to be charged with any crime, he will insist upon having his solicitor present. During this conversation, Mum and Mel are coiled up on the couch both sobbing their hearts out.

Miles is taken out to the police car without handcuffs. Although had he been cuffed, it would undoubtedly have added a little more theatre for the half dozen or so nosey neighbours who are gathered on the pavement looking to dine out on the family's misfortune. It will be a feeding frenzy for all the local gossipers, some of whom probably identified Miles to the police in the first instance. DC Gordon has perhaps been watching too many police dramas on TV as he insists on pressing down on the top of Miles's head whilst depositing him into the back seat of the police vehicle. What is that all about, anyway? Miles has a lasting memory of glancing back towards the house and seeing his parents and tearful big sister picture-framed in the sitting room window as the police car slowly drives off into the distance.

Before long, they arrive at the police station and Miles is immediately ushered into a cold, barren and completely soulless interview room. The room is devoid of any furniture except for a small, cigarette-stained, canteen-style table with three uncomfortable-looking chairs, two on one side with the other facing. Miles is left there on his own for what seems like half an hour, but in reality is probably only about ten minutes. Not surprisingly he is feeling mega stressed. Eventually he is joined by DI Ronald and DC Gordon. DI Ronald is the first to speak.

'Mr Lamont, I believe you understand why you have been brought here today. We would like you to assist us with our inquiries into the death of Harinder Singh on Friday last. For the record, this interview will be recorded. It is eleven-thirty a.m. on Thursday the twelfth of August 2021. Let the record show that present at this interview is Miles Lamont, Detective Inspector Jean Ronald and Detective Constable Andrew Gordon. Let it be known that you are entitled to have a solicitor present, failing which we can arrange one on your behalf. However, at this stage in proceedings, you are here of your own accord and are simply assisting us with our initial inquiries. Firstly, please provide your name for the record.'

'Miles Lamont.'

'And you reside at fourteen Park Avenue, Westwood, London?'

'That is correct,' Miles replies.

'Are you the owner of a yellow BMW sports car, registration number MIL5S?'

'No comment.'

'And will you tell me your whereabouts last Friday evening the sixth of August?'

'No comment.'

'Let me re-phrase the question ... last Friday evening, were you in the vicinity of Bridge Street?'

'No comment.'

'Did you know the now deceased Harinder Singh whose place of business was the Corner Store in Bridge Street, Westwood?'

'No comment. And we can sit here all day and you will continue to receive the same response to all your questions.'

'Let the record show that the interview has now terminated.' Before exiting the interview room, DI Ronald had some parting words. 'Mr Lamont, you are now free to go, but I would suggest that you do not stray too far from home because I have a feeling we will be wanting to see you again in the very near future.'

Miles is out of the police station faster than a toupee in a hurricane.

Chapter 16

'Ok guys, let us examine where we are at,' says DI Ronald. 'We have the CCTV coverage at the train station which fairly convincingly points towards our suspect being in the region of the public phone box. We also know that he drives a distinctive yellow sports car. In addition, we have the sighting by Hannah Wilson of a youth apparently having an altercation with the now deceased. At the moment, we do not have sufficient evidence to proceed to charge Miles Lamont, so I arranged for Hannah Wilson to come in as a significant witness to allow me the opportunity to video-interview her personally. She is currently in the building. Andrew, would you like to accompany me to the interview room?'

Mrs Wilson is a sprightly, blue-rinsed, bespectacled, handbag-clutching figure, probably of retirement age. From having spoken with her on the phone, it is anticipated that when providing a statement she will be very matter of fact with no inclination to gild the lily.

'Good morning Mrs Wilson, and thanks so much for attending at such short notice. Of course I appreciate that you have already spoken to DC Gordon. I would like you to again cast your mind back to events of last Friday. In your own words, may I ask you to state exactly what you saw and when? Please take as long as you like, and please keep in mind that even the smallest little detail might just prove to be of significance.'

'It was around seven o'clock when I drove past the corner store in Bridge Street. I know that because I was due to meet my friend at that time, we were going to the cinema. To be honest, it was the fancy yellow sports car which attracted my attention in the first instance. Then I spotted a young white man apparently having an altercation with an older Asian gentlemen just at the entrance to the corner shop. Rightly or wrongly, I assumed the older gentleman to be the proprietor of the business.'

'How did you know they were having an altercation, Mrs Wilson?' asks DI Ronald.

'By their body language – the younger man was clearly remonstrating with the older man. Also, I heard him – the younger man – shouting at the older man. He seemed extremely angry about something.'

'How did you manage to hear if you were driving?'

'It was a very hot and humid evening and I had my car windows completely open.'

'Did you hear what was said?'

'No, but they were obviously not discussing the weather!'

'By that, are you suggesting that it was a very angry exchange?'

'Yes, that is so.'

'Would you be able to identify the younger man?'

'I think I could identify the one who was arguing with the shopkeeper but not the other one.'

'The other one?' DI Ronald retorts, quite unable to disguise her utter surprise.

'Yes, the other young lad sitting in the passenger seat. Sorry, I think maybe I forgot to mention him to DC Gordon – my apologies.'

DI Ronald glances at her subordinate, an expression that depicts some disappointment in him. 'What can you tell us about the other youth?'

'To be honest, I could not really see his face as he was wearing a baseball cap.'

'And do you happen to know which colour it was?'

'Red, yes, definitely red.'

'Mrs Wilson, thanks for your time here today. You have been

extremely helpful. We would like you to attend an identity parade to see if you can pick out the person in question, and we will be in touch with arrangements.'

Mrs Wilson is then ushered out of the room.

'Ma'am, I have just received a phone message from forensics. Apparently they recovered a beer can from the scene of the crime and there is clearly one set of fingerprints on it.'

'Thank you, Andrew. All the more reason why we would want to haul Miles Lamont back down here. Please set up the identity parade and at the same time we can take his fingerprints.'

Chapter 17

Derek arrives on time for his urgently arranged appointment with his solicitor, Walter Bryson. In the past, any meetings have always been on Derek's home territory; however, in order to access Bryson at such short notice, he has had to accommodate him by slotting him in between his other office-based appointments.

His office is a prestigious-looking, modern, detached building. Derek enters the lavishly furnished reception area, with the expression 'you cannot hide the profits' immediately springing to mind. From the modern solid oak walls to the monogrammed, thick-pile luxurious carpet, it certainly does not disappoint. Having spent ten minutes browsing through editions of Homes and Gardens, the very smartly attired, efficient-looking receptionist ushers him into Bryson's inner sanctum. If the reception is plush, his personal office is quite exquisite with very large windows offering panoramic views to the hills in the distance. After some brief pleasantries, Derek is very keen to get down to business.

'As you now know, my son is in a great deal of trouble. He means the world to Olivia and me, and basically he is a good lad and has never before been in trouble with the police. I will stop at nothing, and I mean nothing, to try to sort out this problem for him. Walter, we are very much in your hands and money is absolutely no problem. I just want to keep Miles out of prison. He is our only son and we desperately don't want to lose him.'

Bryson listens attentively to what Derek has to say, waits a couple of minutes and then in a very considered manner asks, 'Do you literally mean you would stop at nothing?'

'Whatever it takes, Walter. Whatever it takes!'

'Ok, well, what is his story?'

'In summary, Miles was out with one of his friends, Johnny Morgan. They stopped off to buy a couple of beers at a local corner shop. Basically, the owner of the shop was just closing and opted not to serve Miles because he was hurrying to get home to his wife. Whatever happened to customer service and the customer always being right? Anyway, the shop owner then struck Miles who defended himself by striking him back. We can only surmise that the fatal injury occurred by his head striking the pavement.'

While Derek is talking, Bryson is taking copious notes.

'Ok, that's all I require for now. Try to relax, however impossible that may appear. I would invite you to use your imagination. Imagine you have entered my office with the worries of the world on your shoulders depicted by a large dark grey cloud above your head. Then as you relay your problems to me, the cloud gradually floats along and is now above my head in its entirety. And just let's hope I don't get caught in a downpour! I am not suggesting that you can now skip out of my office, but you should definitely be lighter of foot. So let me take care of matters for you. I might not be cheap, but I am good. If, or when, Miles is charged, I will immediately kick into action, and also my meter will start running.'

Interestingly, Derek does actually part company with Walter Bryson feeling a slight load has been taken off his shoulders.

Chapter 18

Today, an identification parade has been arranged in which Miles Lamont will take part. Normally it would involve the witness, Mrs Wilson, being shown video images of the suspect together with eight other people, known as 'stand-ins'. However, due to technical problems within the police station, they are having to adopt the more traditional identification procedure.

Present at the parade is an officer who is not related to the case alongside the defence solicitor. The witness, Mrs Hannah Wilson, is in situ in an adjacent room. The Detective Constables have already been out on the streets inviting various random people to stand in on the line-up with a financial incentive of twenty-five pounds each for the pleasure.

Miles Lamont arrives at the front desk accompanied by his solicitor, Walter Bryson, who is well known to the officers present, even if not altogether well liked.

The line-up is soon in place with a total of nine participants, including Miles. The adjacent room has a one-way mirror which allows the witness to see those in the line-up, but the reverse is not the case. The witness can also speak freely to the accompanying officer but cannot be heard by those in the line-up. The process is just about to commence. However, to the absolute disdain of the officers present, Walter Bryson objects to the process on the basis that two of the stand-ins in the line-up do not, in his opinion, look remotely like his client.

'By law, others in the line-up must, so far as possible, resemble the suspect in age, height, general appearance and position in life. This is not the case here today,' voices Bryson.

The end result is that the officers are obliged to go back onto the street to search for more randoms. In the meantime, the two who are dismissed both appear very concerned as to whether they will still receive their pay-out for having attended. This weighty question is left for others to determine. Allegedly, Walter Bryson always tells his clients to dress pretty scruffily and 'have the look of somebody who would jump at the option of securing twenty-five pounds'. He knows all the tricks, and the last thing he wants is for his client to stand out from the others in the line-up. To be fair to Bryson, irrespective of one's feelings for the man, one can't say that he does not seek every single advantage for his client, however minor.

Eventually, satisfactory replacements are found and the identification parade gets underway. Mrs Wilson is cautioned to take her time and walk up and down the line a couple of times to be absolutely sure. If she is able to spot the man she saw outside the corner shop, she should point him out through the glass to one of the police officers present and also identify him by number.

Mrs Wilson parades back and forth very slowly, as directed. It is interesting that she does not choose to linger opposite any one particular person. Either she is playing the game or she does not in fact recognise anyone. Then suddenly but very assuredly, she stands back in order to view them all in one vista before marching forward, pointing at one in the line-up and stating confidently, 'Number five, I am absolutely sure, yes, number five.' To some extent, she resembles a judge at Crufts striding out to select the winner, except on this occasion, it was the loser.

At this point, all the randoms are relieved of their duties and set off for the local pub to enjoy the fruits of their labours. As number five hangs his head in disappointment, Walter Bryson contemplates a nice little earner!

'Mr Lamont, since we have you with us, we would now like you to undertake a fingerprint test.' As DC Gordon makes this request, there is a reluctant nod signifying consent. 'Mr Bryson, I assume you have no objection to this on behalf of your client?' Having no rational or legal basis for objecting, he somewhat reluctantly agrees.

Chapter 19

It is a normal morning for Olivia Lamont – or rather, as normal as one might expect when one of her family is a strong suspect in a murder case. Derek, Miles and Mel are all at work: it was thought that the distraction might prove beneficial. So Olivia is home alone. However, her peaceful morning is about to be disturbed.

There is a loud knock at the door. She opens up to be met by Detective Constables Green and Gordon alongside two local uniformed officers. They wave a search warrant in front of her before turning her house upside down with apparent scant regard for normal order. This is met by some ranting and raving on the part of Olivia. The complete process takes about three hours in total, during which time they have searched the whole house, garage and garden. They have also removed Miles's laptop and requested that Olivia tell her son to hand in his mobile to the police station within twenty-four hours.

Eventually they leave carrying a few black bags. One of these bags contains a bloodstained shirt which was found hidden away in the bottom corner of Miles's wardrobe. They advise Olivia that all the contents will be duly returned to them except for any which might be withheld and used as evidence in any subsequent trial.

Chapter 20

Miles is again arrested and cautioned, but this time at his place of work.

'Miles Lamont, I am arresting you on suspicion of the murder of Harinder Singh on Friday the sixth of August 2021. You do not have to say anything but it may harm your defence if you do not mention when questioned something which you later rely on in court. Anything you do say may be given in evidence. Do you understand the caution?'

'Yes,' he responds quietly.' He still can barely conceive that this is actually happening to him. This is the stuff you see in films, is this actually for real?

Miles is taken to the local police station where he is read his rights at the custody suite and placed in a holding cell. He is then interviewed with his solicitor present and a request is made to the Crown Prosecution Service to formally charge him. Derek Lamont had urgently arranged for Walter Bryson to be present when Miles arrived at the police station.

Bryson places his hand on the shoulder of his client by way of expressing moral support. 'I will do my very best to have you released as quickly as possible.'

Reality is really kicking in for Miles. He now appreciates that he is not going home to the bosom of his family this evening. Rather, before he knows where he is, he is taken back to the custody suite and placed in a holding cell with other offenders. Can this actually be happening? Is it all just a dream, or rather, a nightmare? I am Miles Lamont, and I have never been in any trouble with the police before – surely there must be some mistake?

Chapter 21

'Good afternoon Andrew, I believe you have an update from forensics.'

'I do, Ma'am, they managed to obtain just one clear set of prints from the beer can which was discovered at the scene, and there is no match with the fingerprints of Miles Lamont.'

'Interesting but disappointing,' replies DI Ronald. 'That leaves us with two possibilities. Either, the prints will be a match for the passenger that Mrs Wilson observed, or alternatively, they belong to some third party unrelated to the case. In the meantime, please look into the close associates of our suspect to see if you are able to secure a match.'

'I have more relevant information from forensics, Ma'am. During the recent search of the Lamont house, a bloodstained shirt was discovered hidden away at the bottom of a wardrobe in Miles's bedroom. I have received confirmation from forensics that this blood corresponds to the now deceased, Harinder Singh. There were no blood stains matching the now accused, or indeed anyone else.

'In addition, we took possession of the mobile phone belonging to Miles. On the evening in question, after the assault, there were numerous unsuccessful attempts by Miles to call his friend, Johnny, and only one call which was actually answered. Also, on the following day there were several other unsuccessful attempts by Miles to contact him.

'Finally, Ma'am, a member of the public – a certain Peter Summers – has come forward to say that he spotted a private registered, yellow BMW mount the pavement shortly before 19.00 hours close to where the attack took place, and it was heading in the direction of Bridge Street where the assault occurred.'

Chapter 22

'Good afternoon, it is Derek Lamont here. Could you pass me through to Mr Bryson, please?'

'Certainly, Mr Lamont, just one moment.'

'Hi Derek, how are you doing?'

Does he really want to know – methinks not! 'Fine, Walter,' Derek says in the hope of rapidly concluding pleasantries. 'When we last spoke, I said that I would do virtually anything to keep my son out of jail. Well, I meant it. My understanding is that you are very well connected and have a reputation for making things happen – and perhaps also disappear. If so, I would just like to say that I am not a poor man and basically, from my perspective, it is a question of whatever it takes.'

'Derek, I believe we understand one another loud and clear.'

'Walter, there is something I would like to highlight to you at this stage in proceedings – something which is causing me no little concern. As I believe you are aware, my son was not alone on the evening in question. In his car was a friend of his, a certain Johnny Morgan. Miles has consistently been trying to contact him, but Johnny is failing to answer his calls. My concern is that he might not have witnessed the confrontation exactly as it happened and therefore his evidence could in fact be damaging to Miles. If you get my drift?'

'Of course, Derek, I understand you perfectly. I appreciate exactly what you are saying. Give me some more details about this young lad, Morgan, and then leave all the worrying to me. In the meantime, I will appear in court for Miles tomorrow morning and will lodge a bail application on his behalf. Although having said that, please do appreciate that the odds are totally stacked against us.'

Chapter 23

The following morning, Miles Lamont is taken to the local magistrate's court, although the case will ultimately be sent to the Crown Court. When he enters the dock, the court is already assembled, the public galleries are full, the press are present in numbers and the magistrate is already in situ.

Beforehand, Mr Bryson had visited Miles in the cells and told him that he would apply for bail on his behalf. Since he has no prior convictions, Bryson would argue that Miles should not be considered a threat to the general public nor a flight risk. On that basis, there would be the tiniest of chances that bail might be granted. However, he cautioned his client that it is extremely rare for bail to be granted in murder trials. While Walter Bryson was in the cell area, Miles observed that he also had meetings with quite a few other accused parties. He was obviously operating within very familiar territory.

As Miles now sits in the court for what seems like an eternity, he is very much ill at ease. He also has the clear impression that he stands out amongst what appears to be a number of low-life perpetual criminals. And yet ironically, he is being charged with the most serious of offences - murder.

Eventually his name is called out. A plea of not guilty is rendered and Mr Bryson applies for bail, stating the case on his behalf.

'Your Worship, I appear on behalf of Miles Lamont and I would like to make a formal motion for bail. He comes before Your Worship as a young man with no previous convictions. He is single and lives with his parents. Furthermore, he has gainful employment. Since leaving school, he has worked for his father in his property company. In addition, my client would happily volunteer to check in at his local police station on a weekly basis. For the reasons stated, I would suggest that I do not consider him to be a flight risk and I would invite Your Worship in this instance to grant the accused bail.'

By way of contrast, the prosecution in turn argue vociferously against bail being granted.

'Thank you, Your Worship. You will not be surprised to hear that I am strongly opposing my learned friend's application for bail. It is an established fact that bail is only granted in murder cases in truly exceptional circumstances. I have been made aware of no such circumstances in this case. My learned friend has said that he does not consider his client to be a flight risk. I don't know what foundation there is for this statement. It seems generally accepted that the accused hails from a relatively wealthy family which, I would respectfully suggest, would actually render him more of a flight risk. The application for bail on behalf of the accused is strenuously opposed.'

A few moments of silence follow as the judge deliberates, then speaks.

'I have listened carefully to the arguments on behalf of both parties, and after careful consideration, I have elected to deny the application.' Then, after quietly consulting with the senior clerk of the court, he adds, 'I can confirm that a trial date has been set for Monday the fifteenth of November 2021.'

When the result of the bail application is read out, it is met with an almighty cheer from someone in the public benches. Miles turns around to see who it is. That someone is Chas Singh.

Miles is quite distraught at the idea of being incarcerated until the date of his trial. As soon as his case is disposed of and before being led back downstairs, he scans the public gallery to find his parents and sister and takes a crumb or two of comfort from their reassuring expressions.

Chapter 24

Johnny lives with his parents. While it is probably not his preferred option, being a student he really has no other choice. However, at the moment this is the least of his worries. The shadow of a court case looming in the future is causing him internal turmoil and distress.

As he is leaving the university campus this evening, little does he know that he is about to face the very worst day of his life, bar none. When walking past the entrance to a quiet lane, suddenly he is grabbed from behind and dragged into it. Before he is aware what is happening, a man wearing a black balaclava has his knee on his chest and a knife at his throat.

'Johnny Morgan, listen very carefully to me. I know where you and your parents live. I also know where your parents work. If asked to give evidence in court against Miles Lamont, you will state very clearly that the victim attacked him and Miles Lamont only acted in self-defence. If not, then both your parents will be very badly disfigured. Do you understand? Tell me you fuckin' understand,' he says as he presses the point of his knife into Johnny's neck, breaking the surface of his skin and causing a trickle of blood.

'I understand,' Johnny mumbles in utter trepidation.

'And if you tell your parents or the police or anyone about our little encounter, then your parents will also meet the same fate as the shopkeeper – and you will have been directly responsible for it.' At that, Balaclava Man runs off into the distance.

Johnny is shaking with fear as he tries to collect himself. He has tears running down his face, tears he has absolutely no control over. His whole world has been turned upside down. He wishes he had never set eyes on Miles Lamont. When he later arrives home, little does he know that his day is going to get even worse.

'Hi, is that you, Johnny?' his dad shouts to him.

'Yes Dad,' he replies.

'There was a phone call for you. I have left a message by the phone.'

As Johnny reads the note, the coldest of cold shivers ripples through his body. He stands there quivering.

'A DC Green phoned from Westwood Police Station. She wants you to call her on the below number. She said it was very urgent – something about providing a statement in a court case.' Johnny's world is collapsing around him. He puts off making the call to the police station until the next morning, a call he is positively dreading.

#

Later that same night, Balaclava Man – minus his balaclava – is at a corner table in the Anchor Bar receiving a brown envelope for services rendered. The donor is a smartly dressed gentleman in a three-piece suit. To any casual onlooker, they would be deemed to be unlikely bedfellows.

Chapter 25

Bail having been refused, Miles is taken back down into the bowels of the court to one of the holding cells. His legs are completely numb and they seem to have a mind of their own, as if working by remote control. He still questions whether this is really happening to him or is he to eventually waken up only to discover that it has all been part of one horrible nightmare? The reality kicks in as he is told by one of the officers that his solicitor will be down to speak with him shortly before he is transported to prison.

Within minutes, he is at the processing counter downstairs and has been asked to surrender his belt, wallet and loose change. The significance of having to hand in his belt is not lost on him. Noise levels are high as officers are bustling about here and there, prisoners are shouting, keys are jangling and cell doors are banging. All this with a view to him being transferred to his new temporary home, pending his trial date.

Miles's meeting with Walter Bryson is as brief as it is uneventful. It consists of him sympathising with Miles that bail has been denied whilst highlighting the fact that he had given it his best shot. By way of token compensation, Bryson claims to be confident about the outcome of the trial and assures Miles that he will remain in constant touch with his dad and that he will also be calling to see him in prison. Finally, he encourages Miles to 'keep his chin up' in a very upper-class, jolly-good-old-boy kind of way. Notwithstanding, his visit has done absolutely nothing to lighten the mood of Miles Lamont.

Shortly afterwards, Miles is escorted in handcuffs to a security van destined for HMP Belmarsh, a high security prison in southeast London. The van is like a sweatbox on wheels. Once in the vehicle, he is locked into a small compartment so small that he feels very claustrophobic. It has one small, high-level, obscured window which does not offer much respite. The van reminds him of news clips where photographers run alongside, holding cameras aloft at its window in the extremely unlikely event of actually snapping a prisoner.

He is truly terrified upon arriving at Belmarsh prison, being aware that it houses some of the most notorious and dangerous criminals in the UK. A heavily guarded, intimidating and oppressive environment, it is surrounded by a very high perimeter wall with guard towers and sophisticated security systems in place. Miles is well aware that Belmarsh has a reputation for being a very tense environment with regular reports of violence and drug abuse. He feels physically sick with worry.

Miles is asked to sign various forms, although it is all pretty much of a blur and he does not even read what he is signing. A very degrading strip search follows, his photo is taken and he is provided with an identity card. This incorporates his prison number, which once again serves as a bit of a reality check. Thereafter, he is introduced to a member of the prison medical staff, to discuss any potential issues. Miles is also provided with the opportunity of making just one phone call for a maximum of two minutes. He is grateful for this opportunity to phone his dad. However, as soon as he hears his dad's voice, he has a complete meltdown and is only capable of uttering a few words amidst his constant sobbing. He is well aware, however, that he is going to have to 'man up' if he is going to survive this period of incarceration.

Dressed in his prison attire, he is then frog marched to his new temporary home in House Block 3-174. There he is provided with the bare minimum of bedding, blankets, pillow, and plastic plate and cutlery. His allocated cell is a very small cell designed to accommodate two prisoners with bunk beds, a toilet (without privacy), a tiny TV and a distinct absence of natural ventilation.

He enters his cell with a feeling of intense trepidation, as nervous as a rabbit in a wolf's den. His cellmate is a burly cement-block of a man in his late thirties, white, large, muscle-bulging, thick-necked with a multiplicity of tattoos. He is currently occupying the majority of the floor space of the cell whilst doing a series of press-ups. The officer unceremoniously announces his arrival as he routinely closes the cell door behind him.

'Billy, I have a new cellmate for you, be gentle with him.'

Billy – or Billy Blacker as Miles later discovers his full name to be – is either deaf or else quite disinterested as he declines either to respond or acknowledge. He simply ignores the fact that Miles has entered his cell; it is as if he does not exist. Due to his large frame, there is no room for Miles to place his newfound belongings on the lower bunk, and so he temporarily places them on the nearest corner of the top bunk. Without interrupting his exercises and without even glancing in the direction of Miles, Billy comments in a gruff monotone-type voice.

'Fuck off – that's my bunk!'

'Really sorry,' says Miles, almost too apologetically as he quickly removes the offending items. He stands there grasping his minimal belongings waiting for Billy's exercise regime to finish. Although virtually no words have passed between them, it is already abundantly clear who the boss is in this cell. Eventually, presumably feeling his muscles are now suitably toned, Billy jumps onto the top bunk, lies down and quickly falls asleep. As far as Miles Lamont is concerned, he is just glad to be able to take occupancy of his own little patch of territory in the shape of the lower bunk.

Chapter 26

DI Ronald is already in the interview room when DC Green arrives alongside Johnny Morgan, the witness who is present as a voluntary attender and can therefore leave at any time of his own free will. He is advised that he can have a solicitor present but has declined. He is being interviewed on tape and under caution. Almost instantly, DI Ronald forms the impression that he is extremely hesitant, apprehensive and not very forthcoming. She does her utmost to put him at ease but unsuccessfully. After some initial banal chat, she gets down to business by advising the interviewee that their discussion is going to be recorded. This statement alone seems to fill him with some trepidation.

'How long have you known Miles Lamont?'

'About six or seven years, I suppose.'

'And how did you get to meet?'

'We met at school and have remained friends ever since. However, he now works with his dad whilst I am at university, so we do not see each other as often as we used to.'

'And were you in his company on Friday the sixth of August 2021? And if so, why and where?'

'Yes, Miles had called me to see if I wanted to hang out with him.

I did not have any plans and so I agreed. Shortly afterwards, he picked me up in his car.'

'Let me stop you there. What kind of car was it?'

'A yellow BMW sports car.'

'Is that with the private registration number MIL5S?'

'It is.' By this point, Johnny was obviously feeling very tense.

'And where did you go?'

'We were just driving around and then Miles decided to stop at Harry's corner shop as he wanted to buy a few beers.'

'How did you feel about that?'

'I was not happy because I thought by the way he was acting and driving that he had already been drinking. Also, I could smell alcohol when I got into the car.'

'What happened then?'

'As soon as he stopped the car, I jumped out and walked home.'

'And how long did that take you?'

'About forty-five minutes.'

'Had you been drinking?'

'No, nothing at all.'

'And did you see Miles talking to Mr Singh?'

'No, that must have been after I left,' Johnny replies as his face noticeably reddens.

'How many of you were in the car, Johnny?'

'Only the two of us.'

'And it's safe to say that no third party jumped into the car when you jumped out?'

'No, nobody did,' Johnny says earnestly.

'Well, what would you say if I were to tell you that we have an independent witness who has stated very clearly that there was someone sitting in the passenger seat while an altercation was taking place between Miles and the shop proprietor?'

Silence follows. Johnny's face is now an even deeper shade of red.

DI Ronald continues. 'In the meantime, what were you wearing on the night in question?'

'Just a pair of blue jeans and a white tee shirt.'

'Oh yes, a baseball cap.'

'Let me have a wild guess, Johnny – a red one!'

'Yes, it was red.'

'Johnny, you are beginning to upset me with your lies. I am bringing this interview to a temporary halt now. However, you can remain here until you feel like telling us the truth about exactly what happened that evening.'

Chapter 27

Given that it has been classed as a suspicious death, a post-mortem is required to be carried out. Present at this procedure are DI Jean Ronald and the coroners officer. Carrying out the post-mortem is Dr Alison Ahmed. All parties are keen that this procedure should be conducted as soon as possible in order that the body can be released for cremation. However, there is inevitably a delay in having these results released as they cannot be published until samples are sent to histology for analysis for drink, drugs, etc.

DI Ronald has now been advised by the pathology department that the post-mortem report for Harinder Singh has been completed and she has arranged to meet with the pathologist, Dr Alison Ahmed, at the local hospital. Dr Ahmed gets straight down to business.

'Harinder Singh was a sixty-five year old South Asian man. He was of slight build and weighed sixty-three kilos. In this case, the cause of death was non-accidental, blunt force trauma to the head. This can produce different types of injury, for example, concussion, contusions, internal haemorrhaging and ultimately death. It would appear that the injuries were caused by an extremely violent blow to the head. In my professional opinion, this was most probably caused by way of a very severe kick to the head. Having said that, I cannot entirely rule out the remote possibility that ultimately death ensued as a result of the impact of the deceased's head hitting the pavement. The histology results did not disclose the existence of any alcohol or illegal substances in his system.'

This report is immediately disclosed to the defence team who then have the option of appointing their own pathologist if they so wish. In this instance, they opt not to, which is a bonus for the Singh family as it would have caused an even greater delay in them securing release of the body.

Chapter 28

Felicity's mobile rings.

'Hi Connie, I had a little feeling I would be hearing from you. You'll have heard the news?'

'I sure have,' she responds. 'Unbelievable – it must be so utterly dreadful for Olivia.' Let's meet up for a glass or two of wine and a chat.'

'Absolutely,' Felicity replies.

#

An hour or so later, Felicity has already arrived at The Grape, a trendy West End wine bar. Moreover, she has made herself very comfortable, nestled into a corner seat with a view of the entrance to watch for Connie arriving. It crosses her mind that such a secluded and private spot is well-nigh the perfect spot for discussing the very serious topic of MURDER!

A mere few minutes later, Constance approaches taking long enthusiastic strides befitting her tall frame and most probably indicative of her eagerness to get tongues a-wagging. They very quickly order a bottle of wine before settling down to some quality gossip. Constance is not one to indulge in preambles and so gets right down to business.

'He could get life you know, Fliss.'

'But Connie, they have been having trouble with that boy for some time, you know,' adds Felicity.

'You are right, Fliss, he is completely spoilt by his parents, particularly his dad, and where does that get you? Imagine giving that lad a brand new sports car at his age. Surely he would appreciate and value it far more if he had to graft to pay for it?'

'How long will the trial go on for, do you reckon?' asks Constance.

'Not sure, but I would not be surprised if it were to take as long as a week.'

At first, Felicity is thinking she is just asking out of genuine interest, until it is followed up with, 'Oh no, I've already booked up my holidays for the year. I'll have to ask for extra time off. Also, I will need a different outfit for each day.'

'Connie, the trial will not be on the TV, you know.'

'I know, but there will be plenty of cameras present and it might be covered by the news channels.'

'Why not ask Olivia if you can sit right next to her throughout the trial as the mother of the accused is bound to be of interest to the press?'

'Good idea,' says Constance, quite oblivious to the sarcasm.

Their bottle of wine is slipping down a treat, so much so that they order a second. In the meantime, both parties seem to be bonding so very well, united behind the but-there-for-the-grace-of-God-go-I banner.

Nearing the end of bottle two, both parties are becoming tipsy and giggly.

'Fliss, see that man up at the bar, the handsome one? He keeps smiling at us.'

Felicity looks up and instantly clocks who Constance is talking about. He in turn smiles over again – and what a smile! He is in his mid-forties with dark wavy hair and very fit looking. He is wearing a crisp white shirt under an expensive-looking brown leather jacket and a pair of Levis so tight he must have had to lie down on a bed in order to close them. Felicity smiles back. Within a couple of minutes, the barman brings them over a third bottle of wine 'courtesy of the gentleman at the bar.' A few minutes later, the gentleman in question saunters over to their table with an empty wine glass.

'I wondered if I could perhaps join you ladies for a drink?'

Flattered by the attention, they both readily agree. He then tops up their glasses before pouring one for himself. By this time, the girls have gone beyond the tipsy stage and moved on to the next stage of intoxication, whatever that may be. Suffice to say that the following morning their recollection of what they had discussed was somewhat sketchy. He introduces himself as Mike Walsh, although apparently referred to as 'Walshy', but is a bit vague about his occupation. However, he does ooze charm and the girls are flattered that he appears to find them attractive.

'I could not help but hear you girls chatting about the murder of that Asian shopkeeper. What a tragic business!'

'Yes, we know the family of the accused very well, and as you can imagine, they are totally distraught.'

Constance and Felicity then begin chatting about the forthcoming trial, the likely outcome and their intimate knowledge of the Lamont family.

From what the girls could remember, Mike Walsh appeared to have some knowledge of the case but seemed genuinely interested in their version of events. Beyond that, their recollection of happenings that evening were somewhat vague. They can just about recall finishing off the third bottle of wine, saying goodbye to 'Walshy' and hailing a taxi to take them home.

Chapter 29

It is his first night in prison on remand and Miles is absolutely petrified. Whereas monosyllabic Billy opts to go to the canteen for dinner, Miles prefers to stay within the relative safety of their cell. When he originally entered the cell block, being so obviously a fresher, he was subjected to a variety of verbal abuse from other more hardened inmates. There is absolutely no point in him trying to act hard or blasé about his situation as the inmates would easily see right through him. He is quite sure he is already viewed as some kind of 'softy white-collared criminal'. So the bottom line is that he would rather starve than run the gauntlet.

His cellmate, Billy, duly returns and promptly jumps onto his top bunk, and before long is grunting and farting in equal measure. Miles feels so desperately alone and so full of regret that one crazy act has landed him in this situation. He is so terribly afraid, not just of the prospect of potentially having to spend years behind bars, but also of the other inmates and the very real possibility of violent acts being perpetrated against him.

Suddenly, the lights go out and his anxiety levels rise an octave or two. What he would give to be back home with his family. He vividly pictures his house room by room and tries to imagine that he is sleeping in his own bedroom, but the protruding and uncomfortable bedsprings tell him otherwise. What he would give for some normality, even to be at home chatting with his very annoying sister. Yes, he is even missing Mel!

Eventually his situation proves too much for him and he breaks down in tears. His sobbing is anguished and uncontrolled. He then abruptly comes to his senses as he is slapped across the face by his cellmate.

'For fuck's sake, shut the fuck up. Do you not realise that by showing weakness you are only making yourself a target for every nutter, nonce and neurotic in this cell block? While I can maybe protect you in your cell, if you go to the showers or the canteen, you will be easy prey for the vultures. This place is a jungle where only the fittest or the smartest survive.'

While these words realise his worst fears, ironically he actually takes some crumbs of comfort in that it demonstrates to him that Billy has something approaching a caring side to his personality.

After a few hours, Miles eventually manages to drop off to sleep.

Chapter 30

A little while has passed since DI Ronald and DC Green left the interview room. If their plan is to make Johnny stew in his own juice, then so far it is working to perfection. He is as nervous as a turkey approaching Christmas. He considers asking to have a solicitor present but wonders if that would simply be deemed as a pointer towards his guilt.

Anyway, why should I feel guilty? I have not done anything, and yet I feel I am being treated like a serious criminal. Does he just tell the truth and hope that the police are able to protect his parents or does he lie, knowing that his parents will be safe, but risk being charged with perjury? In his mind, he keeps switching from one option to the other.

At last, the door opens, another officer appears asking him to follow him to take a fingerprint test. He duly complies. He is then ushered back to the interview room where DI Ronald and DC Green are now eagerly awaiting his return.

'I would remind you that once again this interview is being recorded. Well, Johnny, now that you have had time to consider your position, would you this time like to share with us the truth of what actually happened on the evening in question?' asks DI Ronald. 'Just in your own time, Johnny. Let me assist you with a little prompt. On the evening of Friday the sixth of August 2021, you are a passenger in the car of Miles Lamont and he decides to pull up outside Harry's Corner Store. Let's take it from there, shall we?'

'Ok,' Johnny eventually responds. 'Miles got out of the car to buy some beers. As he approaches the shop, Harry is locking up for the evening. There is an exchange of words but I cannot hear what they are saying as the car radio is blaring. Suddenly, Harry starts to reign blows on Miles who defends himself as best he can. I did not want to get involved and so I ran away at that stage.'

'You are asking me to believe that a slightly built man in his sixties about to go home for dinner with his family suddenly sets about a young fit man in his late teens who is under the influence of drink?'

'Yes', Johnny replies, somewhat unconvincingly.

Just at that moment, there is a knock at the door. It is DC Gordon.

'A quick word, Ma'am, if I may?'

DI Ronald temporarily stops the recording and pops out of the room to speak with him. She returns a few seconds later and approaches the desk, seemingly with renewed vigour. The tape is re-started.

'Johnny, were you drinking on the night in question?'

'No,' he promptly replies.

'Let me ask you one more time, were you drinking?'

'No.'

'And you did not get out of the car at Harry's store and take part in the assault?'

'Definitely not,' he responds, his face reddening further.

'Well, how do you explain a beer can being found at the scene of the crime, bearing your fingerprints?'

Only then does he recall having taken the can from Miles and disposing of it. He then explains this very point to his interrogators, but as he is actually mouthing the words, he himself feels they are not very convincing.

'And why have you not mentioned this fact to me before?' asks DI Ronald. 'Is it because you did not want to let it be known that your friend was drinking and driving, literally? I rather think that this is the very least of his troubles, don't you?'

Johnny rightly assumes this to be a rhetorical question and does not offer any response.

'Johnny, with every passing hour, your involvement in this crime appears to be increasing. I sincerely hope for your own sake that your latest statement is the truth and the whole truth, but I am not wholeheartedly convinced. However, in the meantime, you are free to leave, although I strongly suggest that you remain contactable at all times. You are likely to be hearing from us.

Chapter 31

Walter Bryson has given very careful consideration as to his choice of Silk to represent his client, Miles Lamont, at the forthcoming Old Bailey trial. In essence, he wants someone already known to him, someone whom he regards as being extremely competent but someone not prone to asking too many awkward questions of him. With these criteria in mind, he has opted for Russell Holstein, a young, debonair and extremely ambitious baster who has been making quite a name for himself on the circuit of late.

Bryson and Holstein have already had an initial meeting with their client in HMP Belmarsh for the purpose of reviewing the weight of evidence against Miles. As par for the course for prison visits, nothing is fast, easy or straightforward when making arrangements. The whole procedure is just so time consuming. There is firstly the check-in process followed by the checking and emptying of bags for security purposes. Thereafter, they have to locate a suitable interview room, locate the prisoner and then secure the services of a guard to escort the prisoner. The interview room is itself tiny, barren, soulless and devoid of any natural ventilation.

As far as Miles's legal team is concerned, the case is a relatively straightforward one in that there was a confrontation between his client and the shop owner. The latter lashed out and the former retaliated in self-defence. All the evidence is circumstantial and, provided young Johnny Morgan does not put a major spanner in the works, there is every reason to be feeling optimistic about the prospect of an acquittal.

It transpires that prosecuting the case for the Crown is Joan Calvert, an extremely formidable adversary. She is in her early forties, married to Jonathan Calvert, a defence solicitor, although they have never actually been direct adversaries in court. They would have liked to have had little Calverts, but sadly Mother Nature has had other ideas. Joan is of slim build, very personable and equally extremely popular among both her colleagues and adversaries. Whenever spotted around the courts, she gives the distinct impression of being swift of foot and mind – a legal busy bee. She has a confident gait, sharp wit and an engaging smile. Mrs Calvert is also highly regarded as being very organised and does not like loose ends in an 'everything in its place and a place for everything' kind of way. Suffice to say that Russell Holstein and his legal team might just have hoped for a less capable adversary.

Chapter 32

Walter Bryson has summoned Derek to another meeting in his office to provide an update. Upon arrival, Derek is immediately aware that Bryson is in a foul mood, as evidenced by his opening gambit.

'Who the bloody hell is responsible for speaking to the press?'

Derek is completely oblivious until Bryson picks up the local newspaper and literally throws it at Derek. He looks down at the headline:

"Drug dealer's son on trial for Murder."

Derek continues to read on:

"The trial of Miles Lamont is about to start at the Old Bailey. An undisclosed source close to the family of the accused has confirmed that not only does the accused use and deal drugs, but his father, Derek Lamont, Managing Director of DL Developments, is at the head of a drugs enterprise…"

The article has been written by a certain Mike Walsh. Bryson can see that Derek is truly devastated and also that he has absolutely no idea who has leaked this story. It is clear that it could be very damning for Miles, even though the judge would tell the jurors to disregard anything they have read in print.

Moving on, Bryson emphasises to Derek that Miles need not and should not be made aware there are machinations going on behind the scenes to try to ensure that he is found not guilty.

'It is best he does not know – for a variety of reasons.'

Derek duly agrees.

'It is my view that the case against your son – assuming his pal, Johnny Morgan, does not land him in it – is largely circumstantial. If we were to run with self-defence, it could go either way, but I think we would be alright. What have they got? Evidence he was drinking on the evening in question ... possible evidence of him being a drug user ... erratic driving, mounting pavement prior to assault ... Johnny placing him at the scene of the crime ... a credible eye witness in Mrs Wilson ... blood on the shirt of Miles ... numerous phone calls to Johnny after the assault... I appreciate that this all sounds pretty damning, but it is all circumstantial. There is a distinct lack of witnesses speaking to the actual assault itself.

'Derek, I have some good news and bad news for you. The good news is that we have ways of getting a result. I am "friendly with" and have a good working relationship with one of the court officers. Without me going into detail, let me just say that this could well work to our advantage. Let me also say that indirectly I might well have some influence with the jury.'

'And what about the bad news,' asks Derek.

'The bad news is that all this comes at quite a considerable cost. However, you did say, whatever it takes!'

#

Felicity calls Constance. 'Oh my God, Connie, did you see the local newspaper?'

'No.'

'Remember that guy Mike "Walshy" we met in the wine bar? Well, he was a bloody reporter! He was just using us, Connie. Olivia will be furious with us if she finds out that we've been sounding off. We were flattered that he seemed very interested in us, and all the time he was simply looking for a story.'

Chapter 33

A few days before the trial

Walter Bryson is sitting in a private booth in a traditional, London West End public house where his anonymity can remain relatively intact. He has arranged two illicit meetings in this temporary 'office', the second one exactly one hour after the first.

His first appointment is with a certain Kenny Freeman. Freeman is a short-term 'associate' of Bryson. He is a second-rate, down-on-his-luck, 'do anything for a few dollars' type of private detective who most days of the week is seeking out evidence in messy divorce cases. He is a tallish gaunt man. His face is long, drawn and greyish, partly unshaven with deep-set, tired eyes. It also bears lines, indicative of being a long-term smoker. He wears a suit which looks as if it belongs to a bigger man, an open-neck shirt which was probably once white and a coffee-stained tie. Freeman is to sartorial elegance what Donald Trump is to subtlety.

But then again, Kenny's life used to be so, so different. There was a time, not so long ago, when his life was fulfilled. He was married to Lisa Freeman with a daughter named Hannah and a gorgeous little grandchild named Holly. At that time, he worked in the police force and life was generally pretty good. However, a few years ago, he became the victim of the most terrible tragedy, one you would not wish on your worst enemy. He was on a beach holiday in Spain with his wife, daughter and little Holly. One afternoon, the girls decided to go shopping and left Kenny in charge of Holly, then five years of age. He opted for a few beers in a chiringuito – a Spanish beach bar – where he could keep an eye on Holly. She in turn was running back and forth to the sea to fill up her bucket with water. Kenny got chatting to another couple of English guys, and the ice cold beers were slipping down effortlessly on this very hot afternoon. Before long, all three were pretty inebriated and heavily involved in conversation. Suddenly there was a bloodcurdling scream from a woman in the sea – the type of scream that would chill you to the bone – followed by desperate cries of 'help, help'. Everyone in the chiringuito looked seawards, except for Kenny. He immediately looked to where Holly had been playing but where only sandcastles now stood. His heart missed a beat. He instinctively sobered up and ran to the beach only to discover that the body lying face down in the sea was that of his precious granddaughter. A crowd quickly gathered as the little girl was carried out of the sea. An off-duty Spanish nurse did try to resuscitate her, but it was to no avail. Lisa and Hannah arrived back from the shops just before the police and ambulance arrived on the scene. The shrieking and wailing from Hannah is something that will last in the memory of those in the vicinity for many years to come.

Since then, life for Kenny Freeman has been on a steady downward spiral. His daughter, Hannah, has not uttered a word to him since the incident, and as far as she is concerned, he does not even exist. Also, within the year he was divorced from Lisa. Perhaps worst of all was the fact that he could not live with himself. Every minute of every day he tortured himself, and perhaps not surprisingly, he could not live with his conscience. He had lost all self-respect and on occasions had even contemplated suicide.

The division in the family was never more evident than on the day of Holly's funeral. There was a beautiful and very touching church service. The image of the tiny white coffin was one that would live long in the mind. A casual observer might have wondered why the pews on one side of the church were reasonably well occupied, whereas there was only one solitary soul on the other – one man ostracised in grief.

Now his only friend left in life comes in the shape of a bottle, and of course, this creates its own problems. The most blatant example of this is that within a few months of the tragedy, he was dismissed from the police force for being under the influence of alcohol whilst on duty. Ultimately, he had to earn a living somehow, even if only to satisfy his drinking habits – hence he started up his own private detective business but has to scurry about picking up whatever scraps of business might come his way.

Bryson's second meeting is with Andy Winters – aka Balaclava Man – and his wife and partner in crime, Carol Winters. They have two loves in their lives: firstly, a love of money – and they will do almost anything in pursuit of that goal; secondly, a mutual love of their miniature long-haired dachshund who goes by the name of Oli. Both Andy and Carol have carried out some of Bryson's dirty dealings in the past, and he feels that he can always wholeheartedly rely upon them. Their services never come cheap, but then again, they are the epitome of discretion and Derek did say, 'whatever it takes'. Bryson sets out his requirements to them before metaphorically locking the door of his temporary office for the day.

Kenny Freeman has no sooner left his meeting with Walter Bryson than he is in contact with a clerk of court who works in the Old Bailey, by the name of Michael Harding. The two of them have enjoyed a mutually fulfilling working arrangement over a number of years. In essence, Freeman is the conduit between Harding and Bryson or, on occasions, some other equally corrupt solicitor. In practice, Harding secures not insubstantial financial rewards for providing some very valuable inside court information.

In this instance, Harding is tasked with providing a list of the names and addresses of the potential jurors who will be involved in the Miles Lamont jury trial. The important word in this context is 'potential'. Some of the jurors on the list may well be assigned to another case, others may be dismissed by the prosecution as part of their mandatory objections. However, the jurors in the Lamont trial will come from this global list and at the end of the day, Bryson only has to vicariously target one juror to serve his purposes. Yet in order to achieve his goal, he initially has to spread his net somewhat wider.

After a brief exchange of envelopes, the first part of Bryson's plan can be ticked off.

Later that very same day, Michael Harding provides Kenny Freeman with the all-important witness list which will set the ball rolling.

Chapter 34

Days and weeks have passed by and Miles has learnt to survive in prison. His trial is set for 15 November 2021 and he is literally counting the days with chalk on his cell wall by way of the traditional, well tested gate method. At the moment, he is not allowing himself to contemplate being found guilty: he simply has been unable to countenance that disposal.

His time on remand has been bearable solely thanks to his cellmate with whom he has struck up the most unlikely of alliances. He would never have believed it possible given the evidence of his first day in prison. However, they have been cohabiting very much on a quid pro quo basis. Billy on his own admission is not too hot on the reading and writing front, and so Miles has been helping him compose letters to his girlfriend, his mum and two sisters. In return, although it has never been actually verbalised, Billy acts as his personal minder. It has become clear that Billy Blacker is not one to be messed with in prison and therefore, by association, neither is his cellmate, Miles.

However, this personal insurance policy did not go live immediately and Miles did have one nasty experience early on in his period of incarceration. He was making his way to the showers when he passed another inmate coming in the opposite direction. The inmate in question is known inside as Stan. This is not his real name, but rather a nickname he has acquired because he is considered to be more than handy with a Stanley knife. As he passed Miles in the corridor, he said, 'Who the fuck are you staring at, Pretty Boy?'

Before Miles had a chance to respond, quick as a flash he was punched in the face and then the ribs. As Miles doubled over in agony, he was kicked in the stomach before his assailant vanished as quickly as he had appeared. Miles managed to stagger back to his cell only to be questioned by Billy. The very next day, Miles had an unexpected guest arrive at his cell door in the shape of Stan. Miles was understandably immediately apprehensive. Fear changed to bewilderment as Stan duly apologised profusely to him for his actions. One could only speculate as to what Billy Blacker said or did to create such a response, but either way Miles was mightily relieved. Suffice to say that from that day onwards he was never troubled by Stan or any other inmates and he continued to write letters every couple of days for Billy.

In the longer term, the real concern for Miles is that if the trial does not go his way and he is no longer in remand, there might not be another Billy Blacker to come to his aid.

Chapter 35

Paul and Rita Webster, both in their late thirties, are a very ordinary couple who live a very ordinary life in an ordinary semi-detached villa in an ordinary modern development on the outskirts of Westwood. Paul is an administration manager for a large national printing company. He has worked there since leaving school having worked his way up from being a junior clerk. His life is not only organised but also very regulated and routine, almost to the extent of bordering on having OCD. He and his trusty well-worn leather briefcase leave for his workplace every morning at exactly 7.15 am in order to try to beat the rush hour traffic, and he always parks in the very same parking bay. Mondays to Thursdays he takes a packed lunch with him, but on Fridays he throws caution to the wind and dines in the work canteen. Every Saturday morning, Paul goes cycling for an hour or two, and every Sunday, *en famille*, he pops down to their local, The Pheasant, for Sunday lunch.

Rita is employed as a part-time administrative assistant in a local travel agency, working five days per week from 10.00 until 14.30 pm. The job itself is not very exhilarating or fulfilling and also is not particularly remunerative. However, it does provide the Webster family with highly discounted holidays as a valuable fringe benefit.

The Websters have been trying for a family for many years without success. Eventually they resigned themselves to a barren future and opted instead for a dog. More specifically, a cockapoo, the current go-to breed of the canine world. No sooner have they done so when to everyone's surprise Rita becomes pregnant. Nine months later, gorgeous little Emma Webster enters their world, the absolute love of their lives. Emma is now six years of age.

Paul has received a summons to appear on jury duty at the Old Bailey and is fairly excited about the prospect, not having been called as a juror before. Also, he relishes the idea of potentially having some free time off work.

Little do they know that their somewhat mundane, organised lives are about to be turned completely upside down.

Chapter 36

The trial is fixed for Court Number One of The Central Criminal Court of England and Wales in the City of London, better known as the Old Bailey. It is the largest of the four courts leading off from the marble Grand Hall of the original Edwardian building. The court is steeped in tradition and history, with its rich oak panelling and unquestionable aura. The judge presiding over the case is His Honour Judge Oscar Templeton, a man of great experience and one known for his fairness but also one considered to be fairly severe in terms of sentencing.

His clerk of court, looking quite austere with his wig and gown, announces, 'Court, please rise.' At that, His Honour Judge Templeton appears with a swirl of his red robe and duly takes his seat before opening his laptop.

Early in the morning on the day of the trial, Miles was transferred from the local prison to the Old Bailey. He has been brought up from one of the various holding cells below the court via the hidden stairs to the dock, which is surrounded on three sides by reinforced glass. When he enters the dock, the court is already assembled. The public galleries are full and the press are present in substantial numbers. There is a general buzz of anticipation in the courtroom.

#

Jury selection takes up most of the first morning. One or two are immediately excluded. For example, a young lady who looks as if she is about to give birth at any moment and a man who genuinely needs to be at home to care for his invalid wife. After various exceptions on behalf of both the Crown and the defence, we are left with the following panel of twelve jurors:

Juror No. One – Angela Watkins – a woman aged about forty, married with two children. She is the owner of a small hairdresser business in a London suburb.

Juror No. Two – Julia Anderson – aged in her late fifties with three grown-up children and employed part-time as an administrative assistant in a large distribution company.

Juror No. Three – Leroy James – aged late twenties, single and the owner of a small tattoo artist shop.

Juror No. Four – Jonathon Willcox – aged late teens, single, currently employed as a carer within the local authority social work department.

Juror No. Five – Joy Harrington – a retired lady of indeterminate age but probably in her late fifties or early sixties.

Juror No. Six – Paul Webster – married with one child, an administration manager in a large printing company.

Juror No. Seven – Abdul Khan – aged in his mid-fifties, married with one grown-up child, employed as a foreman in a garage specialising in bodywork repairs.

Juror No. Eight – Prisha Gupta – aged early thirties, married with no children, employed as a legal secretary in a small firm of solicitors.

Juror No. Nine – Bryan Bannatyne – aged about fifty, married but separated, employed as a mortgage consultant.

Juror No. Ten – Elizabeth Flannigan – aged early sixties, married with two grown-up children, employed as a charity worker.

Juror No. Eleven – Stan Adamski – aged mid-forties, married with one child, employed as a secondhand car salesman.

Juror No. Twelve – Albert Patterson – a retired bank manager aged late fifties or early sixties.

This final list had been arrived at after a full morning of questioning the potential jurors as to their background and their proclivities. They were questioned not only about their general views on life but also any preconceived views they might have about being jurors in the forthcoming trial. They were also interrogated to ensure that they had no personal knowledge of anyone involved in the proceedings.

The jury are then sworn in and the indictment is put to the defendant, Miles Lamont. It is quite unlikely that anyone will have noticed Walter Bryson slipping out of the back of the courtroom to make a crucially important call. Judge Templeton then provides the jury with their initial instructions.

'Good morning, ladies and gentlemen. First of all, may I thank you for giving up your valuable time to be on jury duty. At the outset, let me make it very clear that you, the jurors, are the masters of the facts of this case, whereas I am the master of the law. Arguably, you are the most important people in this courtroom. Your task is to assess the evidence and deliver a verdict. It is entirely up to you to determine whether the defendant is guilty or not guilty.'

While listening attentively to the address from Judge Templeton, the eyes of a number of the jurors drift from time to time towards Miles Lamont, as if desperately seeking some reaction or perhaps checking to see if he has any visible horns!

Joan Calvert is also in situ. Her very friendly demeanour and outgoing personality might unwittingly cause one to underestimate her – but at one's peril. In a black suit with a pristine white blouse and dark hair tied up in a fastidiously arranged bun, she is an adversary well worthy of respect. Although known to the judge, for the benefit of the court, she duly introduces herself.

'May it please My Lord, ladies and gentlemen of the jury, I am Joan Calvert and I appear for the Crown, and my learned friend, Mr Russell Holstein, appears on behalf of the defence.'

Chapter 37

There is a little more excitement in the Webster household than usual, given that this is the day that Paul Webster is potentially going to be on jury duty. In truth, he welcomes the escape from the norm.

Rita Webster's administrative job fits in well with her timetable as, being part-time and finishing at 14.30 it allows her time to pop home before picking up Emma from school at 15.00. As per usual, she leaves her house about 14.50 to do the school run. Upon starting up her car in the driveway and preparing to drive off, there is a tremendous grinding noise and she is immediately aware something is amiss. She gets out of the car only to discover that one of her rear tyres has a puncture. In fact, the tyre appears to have been wilfully slashed. Standing across the road watching on but concealed by a tree is a certain Andy Winters on his mobile phone to his wife, Carol.

Rita Webster then gives the school a call to say that she will be a little late in picking Emma up but she will get there as soon as possible. Fortunately, her husband cycles with the owner of a little garage in the town who kindly volunteers to promptly send a mechanic to change the tyre for her. It transpires that she will only be about twenty to thirty minutes late in picking up Emma.

She eventually arrives at the school, somewhat flustered and exasperated, but relieved to be mobile once again. She is greeted by the school secretary accompanied by the janitor.

'Sorry I am late for Emma,' she says, breathing heavily.

'No problem,' says the secretary. 'I heard about your car problem. Your neighbour picked Emma up.'

'Which neighbour?' Rita asks.

'Sarah,' is the reply.

'But I don't have a neighbour called Sarah.'

There is suddenly a hiatus in the conversation, deathly silence as the reality sinks in, then the secretary explains, 'But she said that she is a neighbour and close friend. She also told me that your car had a puncture and you had asked her to help out.' There is another moment of silence as the enormity of the situation filters through their respective brains before Rita bursts into tears and becomes completely inconsolable.

Chapter 38

'But this is not the way to my home. We live in the opposite direction.'

'It's okay, Emma, your mum's car had a burst tyre and I have arranged to look after you for a while. In fact, we are nearly there and I have a great surprise for you, but you have to put this mask on. If you try to take it off to see where you are then you will not get the surprise – OK?'

'Yes,' Emma responds, somewhat meekly.

The car soon grinds to a halt.

'Won't be long now, so keep the mask on.' Carol Winters then ushers Emma into their house and into their spare bedroom. 'Now you can take off your mask and open your eyes.'

Emma blinks a couple of times before opening her eyes only to find a selection of toys and dolls. 'But where is my mum?' she asks.

'You will see her later. In the meantime, would you like to play with your new toys?'

The room consists only of a single bed and bedside table and nothing else except toys. The window is boarded up from the outside denying any natural light. Sarah says that she wants to take a photo of Emma to send to her mum to let her know that she is all right. Emma duly poses with a teddy for this purpose.

Emma watches as the woman leaves the room. She then hears the key turn in the lock and sobs and sobs. She feels scared and insecure and just desperately wants to see her mum and dad.

Chapter 39

Rita Webster is very distraught. She desperately tries to contact her husband, Paul, but without success as he is obviously still engaged in court. She is in a state of total panic. She has phoned the police to report her daughter missing but they do not appear to attach the level of importance to the situation that she demands and that she considers appropriate in the circumstances. The fact that Emma has been missing for such a short time inclines the police towards the view that there will be a simple explanation:

'She has maybe received a lift home from a friend's mother.'

'Has she perhaps arranged to go somewhere after school and you have forgotten?'

'She's only been missing for an hour,' etc....

Rita cannot stand back and do nothing and so chooses to drive home in the hope that Emma has somehow magically turned up there. She probably should not be driving in her current mental state, but she has little option. Upon arriving home, she runs up her driveway in a frantic state – but still no sign of Emma. As she enters the house, she spots an envelope lying on the hall floor simply entitled in large block capitals, 'ABOUT EMMA'. Inside is a note also typed in crude block capitals, the starkness of the message being very much in keeping with its sentiments. This short note will change their lives forever:

> PAUL & RITA, WE HAVE YOUR DAUGHTER, EMMA. SHE IS CURRENTLY SAFE AND WELL. COMPLETELY CO-OPERATE WITH THE CONDITIONS SET OUT BELOW AND SHE WILL BE RETURNED TO YOU UNHARMED, YOU HAVE OUR WORD.

Rita, has difficulty reading further as her excessive sobbing makes it virtually impossible for her to see. She wipes her eyes with a hanky before continuing:

> PAUL, YOU ARE A JUROR IN THE MURDER CASE AGAINST MILES LAMONT IN THE OLD BAILEY. EMMA'S EVENTUAL SAFE RELEASE IS TOTALLY CONDITIONAL UPON HIM BEING FOUND NOT GUILTY AND IT IS YOUR SPECIFIC JOB TO INFLUENCE THE OTHER JURORS TO THIS END.
> IF YOU FAIL IN THIS TASK, EMMA WILL DIE.
> IF YOU REVEAL THE CONTENTS OF THIS NOTE TO ANY THIRD PARTY, EMMA WILL DIE.
> IF YOU CONTACT THE POLICE, EMMA WILL DIE.
> OBVIOUSLY WE KNOW WHERE YOU LIVE, WE ALSO KNOW WHERE YOU BOTH WORK. WE WILL BE WATCHING BOTH OF YOU AT ALL TIMES. PLEASE BE AWARE OF THIS. DON'T TRY TO OUTSMART US. IF YOU DO, YOU WILL BE DIRECTLY RESPONSIBLE FOR EMMA'S DEATH.
> FINALLY, RITA, WE HAVE TWO LITTLE JOBS FOR YOU WHICH REQUIRE TO BE CARRIED OUT IMMEDIATELY. FIRSTLY TELEPHONE EMMA'S SCHOOL AND TELL THEM THAT EMMA WENT HOME TO A NEIGHBOUR'S HOUSE AND ALL IS GOOD AND WELL. HOWEVER SHE IS NOT FEELING GREAT AND YOU ARE GOING TO KEEP HER OFF SCHOOL FOR A FEW DAYS. THEN TELEPHONE THE POLICE, APOLOGISE FOR ANY INCONVENIENCE CAUSED AND SAY THAT EMMA HAS TURNED UP SAFE AND WELL. BE EXTREMELY CONVINCING ON BOTH THESE CALLS. IF YOU AROUSE ANY SUSPICION THEN EMMA WILL DIE.
> FAILURE TO COMPLY EXACTLY WITH ANY OF THE ABOVE CONDITIONS AND EMMA WILL DIE.
> WE WILL BE WATCHING YOU!

Rita is frozen to the spot in a state of abject fear. As she looks down at the note, she spots something else peeking out of the envelope. It is a photo of an unsmiling Emma in her school uniform holding a teddy. The photo has been taken in front of a blank wall providing absolutely no clue as to her surroundings.

Paul eventually returns home that evening with strict instructions still ringing in his ears that he is not to discuss the trial with anyone, including family members. This proves to be the least of his concerns. The very instant he sees his wife's face etched with fear, he knows there is something desperately wrong.

Rita has duly telephoned the police and advised them that Emma has turned up safe and well, and they agree that first thing in the morning they will contact the school with a similar explanation. By complying with these two initial demands, they feel it gives them a little time to consider their next move. They then sit up most of the night discussing what possibilities, if any, are open to them.

Chapter 40

The first day of the trial of Miles Lamont has been pretty much taken up by administrative functions and pretrial requirements. This includes the lengthy jury selection process, direction of the jury by the judge, agreeing of witness and exhibit lists and so on.

The public areas as well as the press areas are particularly busy on day one, and as the trial gains traction, these numbers are only likely to increase. In the public areas are a plethora of individuals each with their own agenda. In one area are Meeta, Aasha and Chas Singh, a number of Sikh friends and family as well as a number of customers from Harry's Corner Shop, all hoping to see justice being done for the Singh family. Also in court, albeit at the other side of the public benches, are Derek, Olivia and Mel Lamont as well as Mel's boyfriend, Stuart. In addition, ostensibly to provide moral support for Olivia – although perhaps more out of nosiness – are Constance and Felicity, both of whom have arrived early to secure ringside seats.

On day one, Judge Oscar Templeton calls proceedings to a very early halt, advising the jury that he is breaking them in gently. Day two commences with addresses to the jury by both the prosecution and defence. These are relatively brief given the very straightforward nature of the case. The prosecution takes the lead.

'Ladies and gentlemen of the jury, my name is Joan Calvert representing the Crown in this case. It is my task to prove to you beyond any reasonable doubt that the man you see in the dock, Miles Lamont, is guilty of the charge laid before you.

'Members of the jury, you have heard the indictment read to you by the clerk of court and you are aware that the charge is one of murder. The prosecution says that the defendant, Miles Lamont, on the evening of Friday the sixth of August 2021 did brutally assault and did murder Harinder Singh at the entrance to his general store in Bridge Street, Westwood. The pathologist who carried out the post-mortem will give evidence during the course of this trial to the effect that Harinder Singh was the victim of a most savage assault on his person, so severe that he never regained consciousness and died in hospital a couple of days later.

'Ladies and gentlemen of the jury, My Lord will in due course provide you with directions as to the law pertaining to this case. It is important that you take guidance on matters of law from My Lord and not from me or my learned friend, Russell Holstein. The law dictates that no suspect is obliged to answer any questions as put to them by the police in the course of their investigation. However, I consider myself to be on fairly safe ground when telling you that you are not entitled to take silence on the part of Miles Lamont as being in any way evidence of his guilt. He has an absolute right to remain silent. The onus is on the prosecution to prove a defendant's guilt if there is to be a conviction. No defendant is obliged to prove his innocence.

'The prosecution will provide evidence that the now accused was under the influence of drink and/or drugs on the evening in question. Furthermore that he became angry when the now deceased Harinder Singh refused to re-open his shop to serve him with more alcohol. This was so because he was already late in going home to enjoy dinner with his wife. We will further attempt to prove to you, ladies and gentlemen, that the now accused in a violent fit of temper, did viciously punch and kick the victim so severely that he ultimately died as a direct result of the attack. The defence would have you believe that the accused was himself the victim of an assault and that he merely acted in self-defence against a slightly built, sober, law-abiding man. Ladies and gentlemen, I am more than happy to let you be the arbiter of the facts. Thank you for your time.'

Russell Holstein now stands to take his role in defending Miles's case.

'Ladies and gentlemen of the jury, my learned friend, Joan Calvert, has very eloquently put forward the basis of the case for the prosecution. However, I would respectfully suggest to you that it is a case built almost entirely of straw. Yes, straw that the defence intends to pull apart, strand by strand. I will show the court that my client, Miles Lamont, is an upstanding young man in the community, a man who hitherto has not had a single brush with the law. Very importantly, I will prove to you, ladies and gentlemen, that any evidence to be led by the prosecution is entirely circumstantial. There will not be a single witness produced by the prosecution to say they witnessed my client striking the now deceased and there is no question of any weapon being either used or found. Finally, the prosecution will be unable to establish any sustainable or credible motive on my client's part. Thank you for listening, ladies and gentlemen.'

Judge Templeton decides that this is an appropriate time to stop for a lunch break with a view to the prosecution introducing their first witness in the early afternoon.

#

The first witness called for the prosecution is a fairly uncontentious one, namely Michael Watson. He is an elderly gentleman, one who so obviously has respect for the sovereignty of the court. He is immaculately dressed for the occasion in a dark blue suit, a whiter-than-white shirt with a complementary blue striped tie and silver cufflinks. This is accompanied by a pair of shiny black shoes, in fact so shiny, one could be forgiven for thinking he was ex-police or military.

Mr Watson was out for his evening stroll when he came across the victim lying unconscious and bloodied in the shop doorway and duly called the emergency services. Joan Calvert takes him through his evidence in a very controlled and measured fashion and the defence team do not see any need for cross-examination.

The Crown then call their second witness, Mr Peter Summers. Mr Summers is strikingly tall. He has dark, slightly sunken eyes, pale skin and mousy-brown coloured hair and a jacket and trousers of such similar toning that they neither match nor clash with one another. His open-necked shirt allows a few greyish-white, wispy chest hairs to pop up to see the light of day. Peter Summers also has a slight glint of devilment in his eye. He promptly takes the stand and the oath.

'Mr Summers, thank you for giving up your time today. I would like you to cast your mind back to events of the evening of Friday the sixth of August 2021, shortly before seven p.m. I would be obliged if you would tell the court what you were doing and if you noticed anything unusual?' asks Joan Calvert

'I was taking my usual evening walk with Deefur'

'Deefur?' interrupts Judge Templeton.

'Yes, My Lord, Deefur as in "D-for-dog". He's my golden retriever.'

There are laughs aplenty coming from the public gallery and one can even detect some guffaws courtesy of Constance. It appears that the public benches in particular welcome a little levity. When the court settles down again, Mrs Calvert continues her questioning.

'Where were you exactly?' she asks.

'I was telling you about Deefur!' More laughter emanating from the gallery.

'Mr Summers, I was asking where you were on the night in question.'

'Oh, I see. Deefur and I were walking along Park Road.'

'And did you see anything unusual, Mr Summers?'

'Yes, a flashy yellow car heading in the opposite direction was being driven erratically and at one point actually mounted the pavement. There were two people in the car, a driver and front seat passenger. The driver was steering with one hand and drinking a can of beer with the other. He was obviously high on drink or drugs.'

Mr Holstein immediately jumps to his feet. 'Objection, My Lord, complete conjecture on behalf of this witness!'

'Objection sustained. The jury will completely disregard the witness's last statement regarding the condition of the driver. The reply from this witness will be struck off the record,' responds Judge Templeton. 'Also, Mr Summers, it would be greatly appreciated if you would simply adhere to the facts.'

'And could you please tell the court, am I correct in saying that this car was travelling in the direction of Bridge Street when it passed you?' continued Mrs Calvert.

'Yes, that is correct.'

'And were you able to decipher the make and registration of the vehicle?'

'Yes, I am quite into cars. It was definitely a BMW sports car, although I do not know the exact model. As for the registration, I cannot recall it, but it was one of these fancy-pants personal number plates.' One gets the impression that Mr Summers is now beginning to enjoy his short spell in the limelight!

'If I were to say to you that the registration number on the car you have described to us was MIL5S, would you be in agreement?'

'I could not say for sure, but it was definitely something like that.' (The fact that Mr Summers is unable to positively identify the number plate does no real harm to the prosecution case as it rather enhances his overall credibility as a witness.)

'And do you see the driver of the vehicle in court today?'

After a little hesitation, he points towards the defendant, before saying, 'Yes, that's him.'

'And finally, were you able to obtain a clear view of the passenger in the vehicle?'

'No, but he was a young lad wearing a baseball cap, a red one.'

'Thank you, Mr Summers, I have no further questions, but please remain there as my learned friend may wish to cross-examine.'

'Mr Holstein,' says Judge Templeton as he invites him to his feet.

'Thank you, My Lord. I will be very brief. Mr Summers, you said the car was going in the opposite direction to the direction you were walking. Is that correct?'

'Yes Sir.'

'I don't suppose that you have extra-special eyesight for a man of your age?'

'No.'

'But you mentioned my client was drinking beer. Were you able to determine the brand of beer?'

'No.'

'So it could just have easily been a can of lemonade?'

'Yes, but I assumed –'

Mr Holstein immediately cuts him short at this point. 'Mr Summers, a man's future and freedom are at stake here today. It is better we deal with facts as the court is not interested in your assumptions. And your evidence is that you could not identify the registration plate.'

'No, but–'

Mr Holstein interrupts him again. 'A brief yes or no will suffice, we don't require a running commentary. I would also like a one word answer to my last and final question – can you tell the court with one hundred percent confidence that the driver of the car was my client, the gentleman in the dock?'

'No, Sir – oh sorry, that was two words.' Once again the public gallery are in raptures.

'I have no further questions of this witness, My Lord.'

'No re-examination, My Lord,' Mrs Calvert adds.

Next to be called to the witness box is Mrs Hannah Wilson. This witness looks fairly austere, dressed in a matronly grey suit with a blouse buttoned up to the neck, heavy denier tights with a pair of sensible shoes completing the ensemble. Her evidence is given in an extremely straightforward manner. In short, she speaks to having been driving past the shop when her attention was initially attracted to a garish-looking yellow sports car. She then noticed an altercation between the now accused – whom she has formally identified – and the victim, but she did not see any violent acts being committed. She also confirms having picked out the now accused at an identification parade. Mrs Wilson, as anticipated, proves to be a very solid, level-headed and credible witness. Probably for this very reason, Mr Holstein once again opts not to cross-examine.

The court then closes for the day.

Chapter 41

Emma is frightened, lonely and bored. She has been left for hours in the locked bedroom on her own. For a short while, she plays with the various toys provided for her but boredom soon sets in. She just really wants to be home with her mum and dad; she is missing them so much. She has no natural light in the room as the window has been boarded up from the outside and it is like being inside a prison.

However, she has formed a special bond with one of the soft toys provided – a small teddy whom she has christened Eddie. She and Eddie the Teddy have become quite inseparable, and Emma has been engaged in many unilateral conversations regarding her current plight.

'Eddie, when do you think I will see Mum and Dad again?'

'Eddie, we have to think of how we can escape.'

'Eddie, if only the bathroom window was a little bigger.'

'I have had an idea, Eddie. When I next go the bathroom, I could maybe smuggle you in under my jumper. Then I could help you to get out of the bathroom window. I could write a note for you to take to my parents. What do you think, Eddie?'

Sadly, Eddie is not very forthcoming.

The woman – she said she could call her Sarah – has come into the room on a few occasions to give Emma something to eat and to tell her to knock at the door if she needs to go to the toilet. Also, she has brought in a television so Emma can watch cartoons. Apart from that, there is no external contact and the hours pass by so slowly.

Chapter 42

Talks between Paul & Rita Webster go on well into the night but have not produced any worthwhile or plausible solution that would work for all – probably because one does not exist. The only really glaringly obvious conclusion is that their love for their six-year-old daughter and only child is completely off the scale.

'Why were we selected, why not somebody else's child?' asks Rita. Then she feels guilty for harbouring such selfish thoughts. But then again, they are currently going through a bitter, resentful stage. 'Why did the school hand over our child to someone they didn't know? Surely this was completely irresponsible behaviour?'

But all this is a discussion for a later date. Their only priority at this moment in time is to secure the safe return of Emma at all costs. If this means that a guilty party goes free, then so be it. Of course they have every sympathy for the Singh family, but if they were in their position, surely they would think along similar lines.

Paul Webster, despite all advice to the contrary, then starts to discuss the case so far with his wife.

'To be honest, I have absolutely no doubt, albeit at this early stage, that Miles Lamont is guilty. It is clear he was definitely present at the place where the offence was committed and he was also in an intoxicated state. Furthermore, he was positively identified as having an altercation with Harry Singh. There is a lot more evidence to come, but there are no other suspects and I think matters will only start looking bleaker for him as time goes on. The only positive from our point of view is that there do not appear to be any witnesses to the actual assault. However, if I think he appears as guilty as sin, the chances are that other jury members will also. The problem is how do I manage to persuade them otherwise?'

Chapter 43

Walter Bryson gives Derek a call. 'Hi Derek. Hope all is good with you. I was wanting to provide you with an update.'

'Go ahead,' says Derek.

'No, I'd rather not talk over the phone as nowadays you cannot be too sure. Could you call by anytime today?'

'Ok, I'll be there within the hour.'

'Great, see you then.'

#

Approximately one hour later

'Thanks for calling by, Derek. It would appear that everything is going according to plan. I am quietly confident that Johnny Morgan will not incriminate your son. Let's just say that we are applying a little gentle persuasion, just from the point of view of focusing his mind,' says Bryson with an almost mischievous glint in his eyes.

'Delighted to hear that,' says Derek.

'Also, we have done a bit of a belts-and-braces job for you. Let's just say that we have a member of the jury who is sympathetic to your cause.'

Derek, appreciating the significance of Bryson's euphemistic turn of phrase, looks visibly concerned by this suggestion. 'But could that not have very serious repercussions on us?' he asks.

Bryson's expression says, 'what part of whatever it takes do you not understand?' However, resisting the temptation to spell it out to Derek, he opts instead for an equally unwelcome and unnerving response. 'Would you rather that Miles were to receive a life sentence?'

Derek is speechless. The bottom line is that he doesn't really care – or want to know – what Bryson has to do to secure the desired result, provided that he can distance himself from it.

Chapter 44

It is day three of the trial and all the usual suspects are in the Old Bailey. One spectator with a very special interest in proceedings is Andy Winters – aka Balaclava Man.

'My Lord, the Crown would now like to lead in evidence, Detective Inspector Jean Ronald.' Joan Calvert addresses Judge Templeton before turning to DI Ronald and asks, 'Good morning, would you please give your full name and job title to the court?'

'My name is Jean Ronald and I am a Detective Inspector, part of the Homicide and Major Crime Command at Scotland Yard.'

'And am I correct in saying that you were in charge of the Harinder Singh murder investigation?'

'Yes, that is correct.'

'And I believe that in the company of Detective Constable Andrew Gordon you did interview Mrs Hannah Wilson?'

'Yes, that is so.'

'And what did she have to say about the night in question?'

'Mrs Wilson had been driving by the scene of the crime at approximately seven p.m. Her attention was at first attracted by a bright yellow sports car. She then noticed a youth having an altercation with an older Asian gentleman at the entrance to Harry's Corner Store on Bridge Street. She also acknowledged the presence of another party sitting in the passenger seat of the car. She was unable to positively identify the person in question, save to say that he was a male youth and was wearing a red baseball cap.'

'And were you later present at an identity parade when Mrs Wilson identified the now accused, Miles Lamont, as being the youth involved in the altercation?'

'Yes, that is correct.'

'At a relatively early stage in proceedings, you were given good reason to believe Miles Lamont to be a principal suspect. Is that correct?'

'Yes, based on some CCTV footage we had secured, he was certainly someone who was very much of interest to us in our inquiries.'

'And I believe you obtained a warrant to search the house where the accused lives?'

'Yes, that is the case.'

'Thank you, we will learn more of this search from one of your colleagues who is giving evidence later on. And did you later, in the company of DC Green, interview a certain Johnny Morgan?'

'Correct – he accepted that he was a passenger in Miles Lamont's vehicle, albeit a somewhat unwilling participant.'

'Could you please elaborate, DI Ronald?'

'He was allegedly unhappy that his friend was driving recklessly whilst under the influence of drink and/or drugs. Mr Morgan appeared to be, perhaps understandably, concerned for his own welfare. He also claims that when Mr Lamont left the vehicle and approached Harinder Singh at the entrance to the shop that he then immediately left the scene on foot.'

'I have no further questions.'

'Mr Holstein, any questions of this witness?'

'No, My Lord.'

After that, the Crown leads DC Janet Green having completed the necessary preliminaries.

'I understand that you were involved in checking the calls to the emergency services?'

'Yes, that is correct.'

'And how many calls were there?'

'There were two. The first was from Michael Watson, the first person to arrive on the crime scene. The second one came from a public phone box in the local train station and this call was of more interest to us.'

'In what respect, Detective Constable?'

'On three counts. Firstly, the fact that the call did not come from the crime scene. Secondly, it was of particular interest that it should come from a public phone box within Westwood Train Station rather than a mobile. Thirdly, upon listening to the call, the caller was obviously in a pretty stressed state.

'Unfortunately there was no CCTV actually incorporating the public phone box, and so I examined footage of those people entering the station in the vicinity of the phone box and then leaving a few minutes later. This narrowed it down to twelve possibilities. Of this twelve, one young man was of particular interest to us for a couple of reasons. It was an extremely hot evening and he had his jacket zipped right up to his neck – which appeared somewhat odd. Also the person seemed very unnaturally agitated.'

At this point, Joan Calvert asks that the tape be admitted in evidence as Exhibit Number One. 'My Lord, I would ask that the jurors be allowed to watch this CCTV tape.'

As they do so, their eyes switch back and forward from the screen to the accused like they are watching a tennis match at Wimbledon.'

'I would now also like to lodge in evidence as Exhibit Number Two, a recording of the telephone call from the public phone box at the station to the emergency services. Also, if it please the court, I would like to play it now for the benefit of the jury,' requests Joan Calvert.

'Permission granted,' responds Judge Templeton and the recording is played.

Hello! Help! (breathless)

...And what service do you require?

Ambulance, you need to get an ambulance.

...What is the nature of the injury?

A man's bleeding very badly. (breathless)

...What is the location?

Outside Harry's Corner Store in Bridge Street, Westwood

...And who is calling?

Just go quickly.

'And did you subsequently look to social media with a view to identifying the person on the CCTV tape,' asks Joan Calvert.

'Yes, we did and the name "Miles Lamont" kept coming up.'

'Thank you, DC Green. My Lord, I have no further questions of this witness.'

'Mr Holstein, any questions?'

'No, My Lord.'

The final witness for the day is DC Andrew Gordon. His evidence is fairly straightforward and to a large extent is corroborating evidence previously heard from his boss. Significantly, however, he does speak to the finding of the bloodstained shirt hidden in a bottom corner of Miles Lamont's wardrobe and Joan Calvert produces it in evidence as Exhibit No. 3. Also, it is established that the blood on the shirt matches that of the now deceased.

'Ladies and gentlemen of the jury, I consider this to be a very natural and logical point to stop for lunch. We will resume at two p.m. to continue with the case for the prosecution.'

'All rise!'

#

Later that same day

'My Lord, the Crown would now like to invite Johnny Morgan to the stand.'

This witness represents a bit of a gamble for the prosecution because Joan Calvert considers him to be an unreliable witness – a bit of a loose cannon. However, depending on how the rest of the trial is to proceed, she equally does not wish to run the risk of the defence team choosing not to call him to the stand. Ironically, although he is a Crown witness, she is hopeful that he will completely discredit himself on the stand. It very much depends upon which version of the truth he opts for on the day.

After the witness has taken his oath, Joan Calvert then steers him through the preliminaries of his name, address, relationship with the accused party, etc. Such information is non-contentious and the defence team do not object to the witness being led.

'Now, let me take you back to the evening in question. I would like you to tell us exactly what happened in your own words, and please remember Mr Morgan that you are under oath.'

'I received a call from Miles asking if I would like to hang out with him that evening.'

'And what did you interpret he meant by "hang out"?'

'Go for a drive, have a couple of drinks, that kind of thing.'

'And did Miles come to pick you up?'

'Yes, he did.'

'And in what vehicle?'

'A yellow BMW sports car.'

'And do you know the registration plate?'

'I think it is MIL5S.'

'And did you notice anything about his condition?'

'Objection, My Lord, this question is too vague,' claims Russell Holstein.

'Absolutely no problem,' says Mrs Calvert. 'I am more than happy to make my question more specific. Did Miles Lamont appear to be under the influence of any substance?'

'My Lord, I must object once again. To the best of my knowledge, this witness is neither a police officer nor a medical professional and is therefore not equipped to answer this question.'

'Objection overruled,' says Judge Templeton. 'The witness is entitled to speculate on this subject and the jury will attach whatever weight to his evidence as they deem appropriate in the circumstances.'

At this point, Johnny looks over towards Miles.

'Please answer the question,' insists Mrs Calvert.

Somewhat hesitantly and reluctantly, Johnny eventually answers. 'Yes, he appeared to be under the influence of alcohol.'

'Appeared?' questions, Mrs Calvert. 'Is it not in fact the case that he was actually drinking while he was driving?'

'Yes,' says Johnny, once again looking over at his friend in the dock.

'And could he possibly also have been under the influence of drugs?'

'Objection!' says an irate Russell Holstein.

'Overruled on the same basis as previously,' says Judge Templeton. 'The witness will answer the question.'

'I have no idea,' answers Johnny.

'Without looking towards your friend in the dock, please tell me, have you ever known Miles to use drugs in the past?' asks Joan Calvert.

There is a prolonged poignant silence, during which Johnny thinks long and hard about his response.

'I will ask you the question one more time, in case you did not catch it. Have you ever known the now accused to have ever used drugs in the past? Please remember, Mr Morgan, that if you are found to be telling lies in this courtroom then you are likely to be charged with perjury.'

'No,' he eventually responds in a very low voice.

'No what?' asks Joan Calvert, more than happy to make him squirm just a fraction longer. 'Please tell the court in a loud voice.'

'No, I have not known Miles to take drugs.'

'Well, the jury will be able to make up their own mind from your demeanour as to whether or not you are being truthful in your response.'

At this, Holstein jumps to his feet. 'Objection, My Lord, I don't...!'

'Withdrawn,' says Joan Calvert, with a wry smile, the object of her exercise having been achieved – namely to plant the seed in the minds of the jury. 'Mr Morgan, how was Miles's driving?'

'A little erratic.'

'A somewhat euphemistic description, would you not say? No need to answer that. More specifically, if I were to tell you that we have already heard from an independent witness to the effect that at one point Miles actually mounted a pavement, would that be truthful testimony?'

'Yes,' replies Johnny.

'Now, please carry on telling us what transpired on the evening in question.'

'Miles suddenly pulled up outside Harry's Corner Store in Bridge Street. He said it was to buy more beer.'

'And how did you feel about that?'

'I was not too pleased because I was concerned about my own safety as a passenger in the car.'

'And did you do anything?'

'Yes, I grabbed the beer can from him.'

'Is that all?' asks Joan Calvert. 'Come, come Mr Morgan, let's get real. There are much more serious issues at stake here than littering.'

'Ok, yes, I threw it out of the car window.'

'Was that upon arriving at the corner shop?'

'Yes.'

'So to be absolutely clear about your evidence here, Mr Morgan. Am I correct in saying that the now accused was sufficiently under the influence of a substance or substances that you felt unsafe as a passenger in his vehicle. Is that a fair assessment of your evidence, Mr Morgan?'

The defendant murmurs in agreement.

'Loud and clear, please, for the benefit of the jurors.'

'Yes.'

'My Lord, I will submit Exhibit Number Four, being a beer can found by forensics at the locus and bearing the fingerprints of this witness. Now, Mr Morgan I'd like you to think very carefully before answering the next question, and I would remind you again that you are under oath. Tell us precisely what happened when the accused pulled the car up outside Harry's Corner Shop.'

'As Miles approached the shop, Harry, the owner, was exiting. They exchanged words then Harry suddenly started to punch Miles who simply defended himself. At that point, as I did not wish to be involved, nor did I wish to continue in the car with Miles, I simply ran off and made my way home.'

In the public area, Andy Winters allows himself a contented smile.

'Mr Morgan, are you expecting this court to believe that Mr Harinder Singh, a completely sober, slightly-built elderly gentleman weighing a mere sixty-three kilos and a pillar of society assaulted a strongly-built youth in his late teens who was under the influence of alcohol? Would you also be surprised to hear that when the police interviewed the now accused a few days after the assaults on his person that there were no bruises or injuries showing?'

Johnny does not respond and Joan Calvert is more than happy to allow these unanswered questions to float around in the air for the benefit of the jury.

'Mr Morgan, am I correct in saying that Mr Singh was stood in the doorway of his shop having just locked the door?'

'Yes, I suppose so.'

'Mr Morgan, please be quite specific about this point as it may prove to be of relevance. Let me repeat the question, and this time, I would like a straight "yes" or "no" answer. This court is not interested in what you suppose might be the case.'

'One more time – Am I correct in saying that Mr Singh was stood in the doorway of his shop having just locked the door?'

'Yes,' says Johnny.

'And so he would have his back to the shop door when speaking with your friend, Miles Lamont?'

'Yes.'

'Good, now we appear to be making some progress. And the defendant was facing the now deceased and would have his back to you?'

'Yes.'

'Now we have heard your evidence today that Harinder Singh was assaulting your friend, who was merely defending himself.'

At this point, Johnny realises that he has backed himself into a corner.

'Would you agree with me that your friend, Miles, would naturally be a much faster runner than Mr Singh?'

'Yes.'

'Well, if Miles Lamont was being attacked, as you are asking this court to believe, why would he not simply run away?'

Russell Holstein jumps to his feet. 'My Lord, this witness cannot be expected to speculate as to what was in the mind of the defendant.'

'Objection sustained.'

'Let me rephrase it for the benefit of the court,' says Joan Calvert. 'Mr Morgan, had you been in the position of the defendant, would you have taken a beating or would you have got off your mark quickly?'

'I don't know what I would have done in the situation,' responds Johnny Morgan.

'The truth of the matter was that the now deceased Harinder Singh was backed up against the door, unable to escape as he was callously and viciously attacked by the defendant.'

'Objection,' shouts Russell Holstein. 'My learned friend is expressing an opinion, not asking a question.'

'Objection sustained,' says Judge Templeton. 'Mrs Calvert, please try to restrict yourself to questions in the future.'

Joan Calvert is satisfied that she has had the opportunity of planting an important seed in the mind of the jury. 'Let's move on,' says the prosecutor. 'There is evidence to show that after the attack the accused tried on innumerable occasions to telephone you and you repeatedly blanked his calls. Why was this?'

'Because I did not want to get involved.'

'I would refer to the telephone records of the defendant, Exhibit Number Five. These records disclose that you did in fact respond to one of his calls. Could you please tell me the nature of this call? What did you discuss?'

'I cannot remember.'

'Come, come Mr Morgan, please remember that you are under oath. In anybody's language, it could not have been termed an ordinary night out. Apart from anything else, it came to a very premature end. Presumably you would have wanted to know what happened between your friend and Harinder Singh? So, what was said on your telephone call?'

'I can't remember.'

'I will leave that up to the jurors to decide what they make of your evidence,' says Joan Calvert. 'Mr Morgan, we have heard your evidence that your friend was being assaulted by Harinder Singh, and not only do you not go to his aid, but you also ignore all his calls but one. Are these the actions of a true friend?'

'I suppose not.'

'I suppose not as well, Mr Morgan,' responds Joan Calvert. 'Is the truth of the matter not the exact opposite of what you have depicted? I put it to you, Mr Morgan, that what you actually witnessed on the evening in question was a brutal attack by your friend Miles Lamont on Harinder Singh, a poor defenceless elderly man. Is that not the true version of what actually happened?'

Johnny Morgan is silent for a few seconds before replying, 'No, that was not what I witnessed.'

'Now, please think very carefully before answering the next question, and I would like a simple yes or no answer. Do you recall when you were initially interviewed by Detective Inspector Jean Ronald that you provided a significantly different account to the one that you have provided today? Mr Morgan, does the proverbial cat now have your tongue? Do you require me to repeat the question?'

'No, I don't need you to repeat the question. The answer is yes.'

This prompts some murmurings within the public gallery.

'Ok,' says Joan Calvert. 'Just to be perfectly clear, you are admitting you have changed your story.'

'Yes,' responds Johnny.

'So you accept you are a liar?'

'Yes,' replies the witness, somewhat sheepishly.

'That being the case, you could equally be lying today.'

'No,' he responds.

'Hardly convincing,' utters Joan Calvert. 'How on earth are we to know which version of the truth is accurate, if any? My Lord, I have no further questions of this witness.'

'Any cross-examination?' asks Judge Templeton.

'Just a very brief cross,' replies Russell Holstein. 'So, Mr Morgan, for the record, your evidence today is very clear and that is that you saw the owner of the corner shop attack Mr Lamont, who then struck out to defend himself. Is that correct?'

'Yes,' replies Johnny, somewhat more confidently now that the heat is off.

'And you are telling the truth to the court here today, and you appreciate the consequences of lying to the court?'

'Yes.'

'No further questions, My Lord.'

'No re-examination, My Lord.'

'The witness may stand down.'

The look of sheer relief on the face of Johnny Morgan is apparent for all to see.

'This now concludes our business for today. My thanks to my learned friends and to you, our jurors, for your kind attention,' says Judge Templeton.

Chapter 45

It should come as no surprise that the Websters are not able to sleep. They each have dark rings around their eyes and they both appear to have aged by a good few years. Not surprisingly, Rita has temporarily excused herself from her part-time job on the grounds of having an ongoing migraine, which coincidentally is not a million miles away from the truth. On reflection, perhaps going to work would have helped her by way of being a distraction. As it stands, she is thinking about little Emma every minute of every hour of every day. And unfortunately, during the day she is on her own, which only serves to magnify the problem in her mind. The fact that she is unable to share her dilemma with anyone other than her husband in the evenings is also extremely frustrating.

Rita is oblivious to the sound of her letterbox opening and closing. It is not until she goes to the kitchen to make a coffee that she notices the envelope lying on the hall floor. She knows instantly what it is, the large block capitals once again saying, 'ABOUT EMMA'. In complete trepidation and shaking with fear, she slowly opens it:

WE STILL HAVE YOUR LITTLE GIRL EMMA. SO FAR YOU HAVE DONE WHAT WE HAVE ASKED, AND THEREFORE EMMA IS ALIVE AND WELL. IF YOU HAVE ANY THOUGHTS

OF CONTACTING THE POLICE, WE WILL KNOW AND EMMA WILL DIE. IF THE JURY CONVICT MILES LAMONT, THEN EMMA WILL DIE. NOT LONG TO GO NOW AND IT IS COMPLETELY IN YOUR HANDS AS TO WHETHER YOU GET YOUR DAUGHTER BACK. REMEMBER, WE ARE WATCHING YOU BOTH AT ALL TIMES.

Rita drops to the floor and sobs and sobs until she has no more tears to cry. She wonders why they had not sent a photo this time around, and this causes her imagination to go off the scale. Have they killed their darling little daughter already? She dismisses the thought as quickly as it comes into her head. She then tries to rationalise. Why would they risk being on a murder charge for no real benefit? Taking a morsel of satisfaction from this reasoning, she proceeds to make her umpteenth coffee of the morning.

As regards Paul, life is just one blur. He is quite unable to concentrate on the evidence of the case for thinking about his precious daughter. He would do anything to get her back safely, and if that means that one guilty party is not convicted, then so be it. Surely any other parent would do the same if faced with the same dilemma?

Often when he should be listening to the evidence, his eyes are wandering around the public gallery wondering if the person responsible for the abduction of his daughter is actually present. Is the abductor actually watching their every move?

Chapter 46

'The Crown now calls Dr Alison Ahmed.'

Dr Ahmed, a petite, dark-haired woman in her mid-forties strides into the courtroom in a very business-like fashion with her file under her arm, looking very comfortable in her own skin and confident in her own ability. She is no stranger to these courts, being very highly respected in the field of pathology.

Joan Calvert invites her to list her qualifications for the benefit of the jury. However at this point, Russell Holstein intervenes.

'My Lord, Dr Ahmed is well known to these courts as being extremely capable and experienced in her field, and so there is no need for my learned friend to run through all her qualifications.'

'Very well,' responds Joan Calvert. 'But for the benefit of the jurors and for the avoidance of any doubt, let me just confirm that in the very simplest of terms that the job of a pathologist is to examine bodies after death to try to determine what has caused the death.' She then turns to address the pathologist. 'Dr Ahmed, on Friday the thirteenth of August 2021, did you examine the body of Harinder Singh?'

'Yes.'

'And could you please share your findings with the court?'

'The body was that of a sixty five year old man, slight in build. Apart from the injuries sustained on the evening in question, he appeared to be otherwise in good health. There was general evidence of bruising to his torso consistent with the deceased having sustained punches to that area. However, the fatal strike was to the side of the head where he had sustained an almighty blow. As a result, the skull was very severely fractured. While it is not possible to say one hundred percent what caused this injury, my educated guess suggests that it was consistent with a kick to the head – one which was delivered with the most extreme force. I would surmise that the blows to the body were delivered first, the victim would then be doubled up in pain and at that point he received the fatal kick to the head region.' She gives a detailed explanation by way of a diagram as to the effect such a fracture would have on the brain and why one such blow would in itself be fatal.

'Finally, Dr Ahmed, could you please state for the benefit of the jurors whether there were any significant findings in respect of toxicology?'

'I can confirm that there was no such evidence, having checked for alcohol, heroin, marijuana and amphetamines.'

'So basically you are telling this court that the now deceased was not under the influence of alcohol or of any known drugs which might have impaired his judgement.'

'That is correct.'

'Thank you for your assistance in this matter, Dr Ahmed. Please remain where you are as my learned friend may wish to cross-examine you.'

'Yes, just very briefly if I may,' says Russell Holstein. 'Dr Ahmed, if my notes are indeed accurate, I believe you said, "My educated guess suggests that it was consistent with a kick to the head." Is that correct?'

'Yes, that is accurate.'

'Is it therefore possible that the fatal injury was in fact caused by the victim's head striking the tarmac?'

'No, extremely unlikely as the injury sustained was not consistent with such an occurrence.'

'Dr Ahmed, I am reluctant to get involved in semantics. However, by virtue of you saying that it is extremely unlikely, this presupposes that it is however possible, does it not?'

'Perhaps, yes, there is the remotest of remote chances.'

'I'll settle for that. No further questions of this witness, My Lord.'

'My Lord, it had been my intention that Dr Ahmed was to be the last witness for the prosecution. However, just a very short time ago and quite out of the blue, a valuable witness has come forward. This witness will talk to both the character and behaviour of the accused which I genuinely believe is very relevant to this case.' At this, Juror Paul Webster instantly feels bile rise in his throat. He puts his hand to his mouth to try to stop himself being sick. There is also an audible sigh from Olivia Lamont in the public benches.

Russell Holstein is on his feet in a flash. 'My Lord, I strongly object to my learned friend's eleventh-hour motion. Whoever this mystery witness is that the prosecution has conjured up at the last minute, I have not had an opportunity to take a statement from them and therefore I consider the defence to be severely disadvantaged.'

'Having listened to both parties and with due attention to the seriousness of the charge of which the defendant is accused, I am prepared to allow this witness. However, I will attach as much weight to their evidence as is appropriate in the circumstances and guide the jury accordingly if necessary,' Judge Templeton assures.

At this point in proceedings, Miles, who has been repeatedly warned by his counsel not to show any emotion, puts his head in his hands.

'Thank you, My Lord. The Crown calls Gerry Smith to the stand,' says Joan Calvert before turning to face the new witness. 'Is your full name Gerard Smith, known to most as Gerry Smith, and are you currently employed as a doorman at the Moves nightclub in Westwood?'

'Yes, that is correct.'

'And were you so employed in August last?'

'Yes, that is correct.'

'I would like you to look to the person sitting in the dock. If he is known to you then please say so and state his name.'

'Yes, I know him and his name is Miles Lamont.'

'How do you know the accused?'

'He used to frequent the Moves nightclub where I work.'

'And did you know a lot of the patrons of the nightclub? If not, why is Miles Lamont known to you in particular?'

'I specifically know him because he used to deal drugs in the club. However, we never actually caught him red-handed until last August.'

'And is that the only reason you know him?'

'No, he was recently ejected from the nightclub not only for dealing drugs but for being completely out of control on what appeared to be a concoction of drink and drugs. I was "escorting" him out of the club when he suddenly turned around and hit me with a right hook, knocking me to the ground and at the same time splitting my lip.'

'And did any charges follow on as a result of this assault?'

'No, my employers did not wish to invite any adverse publicity on the nightclub and they also persuaded me not to take matters any further. However, Mr Lamont was permanently banned from ever entering the club again.'

'Thank you Mr Smith. Please remain in the stand as I would imagine that my learned friend will wish to ask you some questions.'

'Indeed I would,' says Russell Holstein, quickly rising to his feet. 'Mr Smith, I am curious to know why you have only decided to come forth to provide evidence at this very late stage?'

'I have been away on a long vacation and I was not made aware of the case until I returned.'

'I put it to you that you are making up this story about Mr Lamont.'

'I can assure you that is not true. If you don't believe me, ask his friend Johnny Morgan – he was with him that night. I have only decided to provide evidence in this case because I am very anti-drugs given that my young sister died of an overdose a few years ago.'

At this point, Russell Holstein realises that his cross-examination is probably causing more harm than good. 'No further questions of this witness, My Lord.'

Joan Calvert jumps to her feet. 'No re-examination, My Lord. That concludes the case for the Crown.'

'Very well,' says Judge Templeton, 'we will continue tomorrow morning with the case for the defence.'

Chapter 47

Immediately after the prosecution closes their case on behalf of the Crown, Russell Holstein lets Miles know that he and Mr Bryson will be following him down to the cell area to discuss how the case has been proceeding and what their tactics should be going forward. Derek is also wanting to be in on the meeting, but Walter Bryson discourages him on the basis that Miles might be a little less forthcoming if his dad were present. However, Derek insists and Bryson eventually withdraws his resistance.

So, within a half hour or so of the court finishing for the day, all four of them squeeze into a tiny, bare, stuffy cell and Russell Holstein immediately takes the lead.

'Ok, you will obviously be wanting my view on how the trial is going. Well, I was reasonably pleased with the way things were proceeding, that is until we were derailed at the last minute by their final witness, Gerry Smith. That was a bit of a body blow to our case. Not only did it show that you were involved with drugs, speaking to your character, but more importantly that you had previously displayed violent tendencies. Notwithstanding this slightly damning eleventh-hour evidence, the case against you is still nevertheless all circumstantial. The question is what weight will the jury attach to all these strands of evidence? On balance, I do not believe there is enough to convict you, but there are never any guarantees. I know this well from years of experience.'

At this point, Derek has his say. 'So at the moment, you are saying that the scales are very slightly weighed in our favour. Surely once you lead evidence for the defence, we will have even more of an edge? Miles will present well on the stand and could influence jurors in our favour.'

'Derek,' Holstein responds. 'Please believe me that there is nothing the Crown would like better than for your son to take the stand as they would look forward to tearing him apart. I can imagine them getting under his skin as they continually question him on his drugs involvement and his drinking. Also, the Crown would rejoice in the opportunity of bringing up the violent incident at the nightclub.'

At this point, Miles contributes. 'I agree with Dad that I should give evidence so that the jurors can hear my side of the story.'

'Very well,' says Holstein. 'Your dad is paying me a not-insubstantial sum to represent your interests and to provide you with the benefit of my experience and expertise. Forgive me if I am stating the obvious, but you must appreciate that there is absolutely no obligation on the defence to lead evidence. Furthermore, it is for the Crown to prove the case against you beyond any reasonable doubt – which is quite an exacting standard. I suggest that you sleep on it and reserve your final decision until the morning, but please, in your own interests, do think extremely carefully about what I have said.

'Also, I see no point in leading any character witnesses. Firstly, I have my doubts about their effectiveness with a jury – as even a mass murderer could find someone to speak positively about them. However, much more importantly, if we lead a character witness, my fear is that it opens the door for the Crown to once again cross-examine the witness and this might just invite evidence we would not wish to come out into the open.'

Before leaving the cells area, Walter Bryson asks for a quiet word with Derek. 'I have told you already that we have someone within the jury fighting the fight for us. Trust me, Derek, allowing Miles to give evidence is simply playing into the hands of the prosecution. They would be rubbing their hands with glee. If you really meant whatever it takes, well this is a part of it. I need you to make sure that you convince Miles not to give evidence, without of course mentioning our potential influence on the jury and a witness.'

Chapter 48

A half hour or so before the trial is scheduled to re-commence, Bryson and Holstein are still trying to persuade Miles not to give evidence.

'But they will surely want to hear my side of the story?' Miles pleads. 'If I don't give evidence, the jurors will just think I'm guilty.'

Walter Bryson is fairly blunt in his response. 'Miles, if you were wanting your appendix taken out, would you do it yourself or leave it to a medical specialist?' It was a rhetorical question. 'Well, why not put your trust in two experienced professionals in the legal field to save you spending years in jail. Yes, of course we cannot give you any guarantees, but we can so influence the odds in your favour.'

#

'Court Rise!'

'Good morning to you all. My recollection is that in yesterday's session we adjourned at a very convenient time, namely the conclusion of the Crown case. So, ladies and gentlemen of the jury, the defence team now have the opportunity of leading evidence on behalf of the accused. Mr Holstein,' says Judge Templeton.

'Thank you, My Lord, but after careful consideration, we have decided not to lead any evidence on behalf of the defence.' This causes some murmurings from the public benches.

The defendant had been asked by Mr Holstein to wear a suit and shirt and tie each day. But he is now truly regretting it as he is literally feeling very hot under the collar. He keeps tugging at his collar in an attempt to breathe more freely and feels in need of an oxygen supply. The reality has now truly kicked in – just two more presentations to the court and then it goes to the jury – there will be nothing else that can be done for him. He glances up at the public gallery and notices the steely eyes of Chas bearing down on him.

'Mrs Calvert, you were not to know that the defence wasn't going to be leading evidence. Accordingly, do you require more time before your final submission or are you ready to go?'

'Ready to go, My Lord.'

'Mr Holstein, I trust you are too?'

'Yes, My Lord.'

Judge Templeton then addresses the jurors. 'Ladies and gentleman, in case you are not acquainted with court procedure, Mrs Joan Calvert on behalf of the Crown will now make final submissions to you followed by Mr Russell Holstein on behalf of the defence. I would imagine these will be concluded within an hour or two. I will then address you. Thereafter, you will be invited to commence your deliberations.'

Chapter 49

'Mrs Calvert, the floor is yours.'

'Thank you, My Lord. Ladies and gentlemen of the jury, as Judge Templeton has said, I am now about to state the case for the prosecution. Let me say at the very outset that by comparison with the cases I deal with on a daily basis, this is a very straightforward one.

'The defence has exercised their right not to lead evidence, as they are entirely entitled to do. So we have not heard any evidence from any witness suggesting that someone else other than the accused carried out an assault on the victim, Harinder Singh. Nor has there been any evidence to suggest that it has all been a case of mistaken identity. Had it been so, then the accused would have had an alibi to put forward to the court. So, I don't think there is any doubt in our minds that the accused had an altercation with the victim. During the trial, there has been the suggestion from my learned friend of a defence of self-defence. I would submit to you that this is mere fantasy for the following reasons.

'One – You have heard in evidence that the victim is a slightly built man in his sixties and a pillar of society. Is the defence genuinely expecting you to believe that the late Harinder Singh was the aggressor? Had he been, no doubt my learned friend would have introduced photographic evidence of his client's battle wounds – but not so. I would suggest to you, ladies and gentlemen, this is because Mr Lamont did not have any injuries because he was the aggressor who viciously punched and kicked his victim, ultimately causing loss of life.

'Two – you will recall me questioning the witness, Johnny Morgan, regarding the relative physical positions of the defendant and the victim in the doorway. The witness eventually admitted, albeit with considerable reluctance, that the defendant could easily have escaped had he been subjected to an attack, but he chose not to take that course of action.

'Three – And what of motive? What possible motive would the victim have for assaulting one of his customers? Absolutely none! He was a family man about to close up his family business in order to go home to his loving wife. As for the accused, it seems quite clear that he was one angry man because he wanted more beer and he was being denied that pleasure.

'Four – We have also heard evidence from Johnny Morgan that the accused was under the influence of a substance or substances. It might have been just alcohol or else a concoction of drugs and alcohol, but I guess we will never know for sure. Ladies and gentlemen, I honestly do not need to point out what an unreliable witness Johnny Morgan has been and he might well be facing charges after this trial for perjury. However, what was obvious to us all was that he was trying to help his pal out wherever he could. On that basis, I would somewhat ironically suggest to you that the evidence from him regarding the defendant being under the influence is all the more credible. Then again, there is also very significant testimony from Peter Summers who speaks to the erratic driving by the accused shortly before the attack. By comparison, the post-mortem report on the victim shows the complete absence of any such substances.

'Five – And of course the accused took off after the attack with no apparent concern for his victim bleeding out on the street. Eventually, he did make a phone call but only anonymously after he felt he was a safe distance away from the scene of the crime. Had he not been only thinking of himself and had he acted more quickly, Mr Harinder Singh might still be with his family here today.' This comment prompts a few sobs from the public benches.

'Six – You have heard evidence that the accused repeatedly tried phoning his pal, Johnny Morgan, after the assault and all but one call he refused to answer. Why would he be so desperate to speak to him? I feel it would not be unreasonable to assume it was with a view to ensuring that their stories corroborated one another. As to that one phone call, if you are to believe the testimony of Johnny Morgan, he is unable to recall what was said.

'Seven – Late on in proceedings, we heard from the witness Gerry Smith who spoke to the character of the accused. In particular, not only did he make mention of the accused taking drugs but also dealing in drugs. Even more damning was the evidence he gave the court establishing that Miles Lamont also had a predisposition to violence.

'Eight – Ladies and gentlemen, there is of course the icing on the cake. The accused went home after the assault, took off his bloodstained shirt and wilfully concealed it in the bottom corner of his wardrobe, obviously not anticipating that the police would have a warrant to search his house quite so quickly, if at all. Let me emphasise one point due to its great significance. Ladies and gentlemen, you all saw the blood-covered shirt that was produced during the trial. I would suggest that you might think it extremely significant that there was not one single speck of blood of the accused on his shirt or anywhere for that matter.

'Ladies and gentlemen of the jury, I have detained you quite long enough. I have just presented to you the facts, not opinions. Each of these eight threads of evidence are pretty damning on their own, but when woven together, they create a tapestry – a tapestry of guilt. So I would ask you to consider very carefully the points I have raised and return a unanimous verdict of guilty – guilty of the charge of murder. You owe it to the court, and you owe it to the Singh family.' At that very moment, Joan Calvert looks benignly towards the family of the deceased in the public benches whilst once again deliberately letting her words hang in the air.

'I thank you all once again for your time and attention and have every confidence that you will ultimately arrive at the right decision.'

Chapter 50

'Over to you,' says Judge Templeton to Russell Holstein.

'Thank you, My Lord,' he voices whilst rising to his feet. He then walks very slowly and very purposefully over to where the jurors are sitting. With each short stride, he is demanding more and more attention from his audience of twelve. When he reaches them, he suddenly stops in his tracks, somewhat dramatically pirouettes on his heels and then stares at the accused. He is revelling in the theatre.

All the while, rivulets of sweat are making their way down the face of Paul Webster by a variety of routes, the more ambitious ones opting for his nose and then jumping for freedom from there in true Eddie the Eagle style.

'Ladies and Gentlemen of the jury, I would now like to address you on behalf of the defence.' At this point, he once again goes silent for a moment or two for dramatic effect. He then stands with his legs apart and his arms outstretched on the ledge in front of the jurors. Paul Webster is sitting two places from the right in the front row, so close to the defence barrister he can tell he had garlic for his dinner the previous night. Paul allows the very random thought to enter his mind that this might just alienate the jurors. Stress and anxiety can affect people in the strangest of ways as he almost allows himself a slight smile.

'Ladies and gentlemen, given that it is very warm in the courtroom today, you might be pleased to hear that I will try to detain you for as short a time as possible, basically because there is no real case to answer.

'May I begin by complimenting my learned friend for her most eloquent and persuasive address. She made mention of weaving threads and creating a tapestry – extremely erudite. However, I would respectfully suggest that her choice of metaphor is more than a little inaccurate. I would rather suggest that the Crown case is made out of straw.

'I am not going to go through every little strand of evidence led by the Crown – there is no point as they are all very circumstantial. Rather, I will fairly succinctly address the real evidence in this case.

'Ladies and gentlemen, let me make something abundantly clear to you. The case for the prosecution is all smoke and mirrors. The bottom line is that not a single one of the witnesses that we have heard give evidence for the Crown actually witnessed an assault on Harinder Singh. Is there any one of you on this jury who can honestly say that you know for sure what happened between Harinder Singh and my client that fateful evening? No, you don't because it is all supposition.' Holstein then hesitates for more dramatic effect before appearing to make eye contact with each and every juror before continuing. 'If it were your son sitting in the dock, a young man with no previous criminal convictions, how would you feel if he were to be locked up for several years based on supposition? I think we all know the answer. Please keep this thought uppermost in your mind whilst making your deliberations.

'I thank you for your time and for listening to me so attentively and I trust you will conclude that there is only one true and just verdict – not guilty.'

Chapter 51

'Ladies and gentlemen, thank you for sitting so patiently through the evidence in this case and also to the closing arguments of counsel for the Crown and the defence. It is now my turn as presiding judge to address you to ensure that you are fully aware of the very important and invaluable role that you have to play in this process. You are in fact the most significant people in this courtroom,' says Judge Oscar Templeton as he addresses the court.

'The judge and jury in a criminal trial have two completely different functions. I am the master of the law, and any directions in law given by me, you must accept and apply to the case. By comparison, you, the jury, are the master of the facts and moreover are the sole arbiters of the facts of the case.

'Let me first clarify for you the concept of burden of proof. The prosecution must prove its case against the defendant. The defendant is innocent until proven guilty. It is not for the defendant to prove he is innocent but for the prosecution to prove he is guilty. In this particular case, the defence has chosen not to place the accused in the witness box. They are completely entitled to make such a decision. Furthermore, nor should any inference be taken from the defendant's decision not to give evidence in these proceedings. This is entirely his right.

'As well as the burden of proof, I would like to address you on the standard of proof. To prove that a defendant is guilty, the prosecution must prove its case beyond reasonable doubt,often referred to as making the jury "satisfied so that they are sure" of the defendant's guilt.This is not to be interpreted as a whimsical or fanciful doubt, but a reasonable one. This is the standard of proof.

'If after hearing the evidence the jury are less than convinced, then the defendant is entitled to be acquitted, namely found not guilty. This means that even if a jury think a defendant is probably guilty but are not sure of his/her guilt, the correct verdict should be one of not guilty.

'Let me now revert to the particular facts of this case which are relatively straightforward. There is little doubt that on the evening in question an altercation took place between the victim and the defendant. In essence, the case for the Crown is that the defendant who was under the influence of drink viciously assaulted the now deceased. By contrast, the defence has suggested that the now accused was being assaulted by Harinder Singh and merely struck out in self-defence. Based on the facts before you, it is up to you to decide which version represents the true facts of the case.

'Let me now go into a little more detail regarding the law in self-defence cases. A man who is attacked or believes that he is about to be attacked may use such force as is both necessary and reasonable in order to defend himself. If that is what he does, then he acts lawfully. It follows that a man who starts the violence, the aggressor, cannot rely upon self-defence to render his actions lawful.

'Members of the jury, I'm going to send you out to begin your deliberations. Please take just as long as you feel is necessary. A court may now accept a majority verdict from a jury in certain circumstances. Should this situation arise, I will bring you back into court and give you a further direction. However, at this point in time, my instruction to you is that you must seek a unanimous verdict. By unanimous, of course, I mean a verdict upon which all twelve of you are agreed. Firstly, you require to appoint a foreperson from among your midst. The foreperson's main job is to chair discussions in the jury room and to return the verdict when you return to court. In addition, during your deliberations, should you have any queries or concerns then it is the job of the foreperson to bring this to my attention via the court officer. Also, please be informed that during your retirement, any exhibits you may wish to revisit will be made available to you.'

Generally speaking, a judge's address to the jury can be rather mundane or boring and they run the risk of one or two of the jurors dropping off to sleep. But this group of jurors are being extremely diligent with the majority of them taking notes. In reality, it is impossible to decipher from their facial expressions which way they are likely to vote, but that does not stop the onlookers playing the game.

'Ladies and gentlemen of the jury, I now discharge you to carry out your deliberations. Thank you for your attention and remember, please do not discuss this case with anyone else other than your fellow jurors.'

Chapter 52

Walter Bryson and Russell Holstein have sat through many a jury trial and usually have a fair idea of which way a jury is leaning. Here, everything points towards Miles being guilty, but there are no actual witnesses to the assault, or at least none that have come forward.

'If ever there was a case which is hanging on reasonable doubt, then this is it,' states Walter Bryson. 'I think we have in the bag juror number one, the woman who owns the hairdresser business. Also juror number three, Tattoo Man, and juror number four, Jonathan Willcox, the local authority care worker. Juror number six, Paul Webster, also seems sympathetic to our cause. Juror number seven, Abdul Khan, the garage foreman, might be with us, but I am just not too sure about him.

'By contrast, I would say that most definitely in the prosecution camp are the following – juror number five, Joy Harrington, and juror number twelve, Albert Patterson, the retired bank manager. Also kicking for the opposing team are juror number nine, Bryan Bannatyne, the mortgage consultant, and juror number eleven, Stan Adamski, the secondhand car salesman. As for the others, they are anybody's guess, and they are the ones who will ultimately determine the final verdict.'

One by one, the twelve jurors file into the austere, traditional, oak-panelled jury room and Paul is feeling as nervous as a long-tailed cat in a room full of rocking chairs. Eventually all twelve 'disciples' are in place, but little do they know they have a Judas in their midst. Paul decides that his interests would best be served by him immediately taking the initiative by throwing his hat in the foreperson ring.

'Hi all, let us get down to business right away. Our first function is for us to appoint a foreperson. My name is Paul Webster, I am married with one child and work as an administration manager in a printing company in London. I would like to put myself forward as the foreperson.' There is a short silence during which he is conscious that all eyes are fixed on him. He is just envisaging that he might be appointed unopposed when juror number five raises her hand.

'I, too, would like to put myself forward.' The raised hand belongs to a certain Joy Harrington. She provides a little background. 'I am retired but have a few years recent experience of working voluntarily as a committee member for a national charity which would hopefully hold me in good stead.'

Joy is a lady of indeterminate age. If forced to guess, I would suggest late fifties, perhaps early sixties, wearing a red knitted cardigan over a cream blouse buttoned up to her neck, a long skirt down to her ankles, a sturdy pair of ankle boots, very large circular earrings and a subtle nose piercing. She could be described as being very vaguely bohemian in appearance. It would be no great surprise to discover that she is a committed member of her local library and a paid-up member of the lifeboat society. For sure, she is a woman not short of self-confidence and a credible adversary. Things are only about to get worse as a third contender intimates interest in the role.

'My name is Albert Patterson and I am a retired bank manager. I, too, would like to put my name forward.' If you had not known this juror's past occupation, one could reasonably have had a pretty good guess at it. Aged probably in his late fifties or early sixties, he is attired in an immaculate grey suit with a pristine white shirt and a grey and white striped tie. His shirt is so beautifully pressed one could have been forgiven for thinking that he had fallen asleep on a hanger. On his left lapel are two discreet badges, one representing the local rotary club, the other depicting English Heritage. During the jury selection procedure, he was the very last to be selected, by which time the defence had – unfortunately for them – already used up all their mandatory objections. So sadly, Albert Patterson has slipped through the net as far as the defence team are concerned as they would definitely have objected to this juror if at all possible.

Once again, trying to appear like a natural leader and an organised type of individual, Paul opts to take the initiative.

'Well, it would appear that we have three potential forepersons in our midst. I propose the fairest way to deal with this is by secret ballot.' He immediately starts tearing an A4 sheet into twelve equal pieces and distributes them. 'May I ask you each to take one and write either "Joy", "Albert" or "Paul" on it, fold it up and then place it in this glass jar. It is quite in order to vote for yourself.' All duly comply. 'Whoever has the fewest votes will not be elected foreperson and then we will have a further vote between the remaining two.' Paul swirls the contents of the glass jar and then select the names, one by one:

Albert
Albert
Joy
Paul
Joy
Paul
Paul
Joy
Albert
Albert
Paul
Paul

'Based on these results, Joy is now eliminated from the voting process.' Paul is trying not to show the relief on his face, but so far, he has only won the battle, not the war. He is distracted as his thoughts go to his precious daughter, and he envisages Emma's face and wonders what she is doing at that very minute. He then tears up yet more strips of paper and declares the results of the second and final draw:

Paul
Paul

Paul
Albert
Albert
Paul
Albert
Albert
Albert
Paul
Albert
Albert

Almost in a trance, Paul then announces the 7-5 result in favour of Albert and formally declares him to be the jury foreperson. He tells himself that this is merely a small hiccup along the way and one that can easily be overcome. He simply has to believe this to be the case, for his own sanity.

'Ok, let's get started,' says Albert, immediately appearing to revel in his newly found status. 'We have all heard the evidence and the addresses on behalf of both the prosecution and the defence. In order to start the ball rolling, I think we should have a show of hands of those who would favour a vote of guilty, those who would vote not guilty and finally those who are as yet undecided. Those for guilty?'

Albert shoots his hand in the air as do two others.

'Not Guilty?'

Paul Webster and three others raise their hands.

'Undecided?'

Five other hands are raised, including Joy Harrington's.

'Seems like we are going to have a lot to talk about. But first of all, we are being re-called to court.'

Chapter 53

Once everyone else is in situ, the jury is called back into court towards the end of the afternoon session. The clerk of court bows in front of Judge Templeton before inviting the accused to stand, followed by the foreperson, Albert Patterson. Albert has changed his seat position as he is now strategically located in the front row of the jury, closest to the bench. The judge then addresses the foreperson.

'Has the jury reached a verdict on which you are all agreed?'

'As yet, we have failed to reach a unanimous decision,' says the newly appointed foreperson.

'I will therefore have to ask you to retire once again and strive to reach a unanimous decision. However, if you are still not able to arrive at a unanimous verdict, then I am prepared to accept a majority verdict. But let me explain that the law of the country will allow me to accept a majority verdict only if it is one on which no less than ten members of the jury are in agreement.

'Mr Foreperson,' continues Judge Templeton, 'it is not for me to know as to how the jury is divided, nor should you advise me of same. But I am fully entitled to ask you one question. If I were to allow your considerations to continue further, would you believe it reasonable to suppose that a verdict acceptable to this court might be arrived at?'

'Hopefully, My Lord.'

At this point, the jury members are formally discharged in order to enable them to continue their deliberations. But ringing in their ears is a strict reminder from Judge Templeton not to discuss the case with any third party.

Chapter 54

Despite now being surrounded by colouring books as well as toys, Emma is bored, lonely and desperately missing cuddles and love from her mum and dad. She is often crying herself to sleep. The woman, 'Sarah' is nice enough to her but is absolutely no substitute for her own family. Also, why does she have to be restricted to the one room and be escorted to the bathroom any time she needs to go? She longs for her own room, her own toys and most of all her favourite doll called Daisy. She had asked Sarah if she could get Daisy for her but was told no. She is grateful for having Eddie the Teddy, but he is no real substitute for Daisy. However, she looks forward to eventually being able to introduce them to one another at some time in the future.

She has not been told why she has been taken away from her parents nor does she think she has done anything really bad. A few days ago, Mum had asked her to tidy up her room but she had forgotten. She wonders whether being locked into this room in a strange house could be her punishment. But no, her parents would never be so cruel. Each day she asks Sarah if she will take her home, and each day she says, 'tomorrow' but somehow tomorrow never seems to arrive.

Carol Winters is also going stir crazy cooped up in the same house day after day. It is okay for her husband, Andy, as at least he is experiencing the drama of the courtroom from the public benches. However, whenever she is feeling at her lowest ebb, she thinks of the mega babysitting fee coming her way. This somehow manages to strengthen her resolve while settling down to watch yet another episode in the 'A Place in the Sun' daytime TV series, all the while imagining how exactly she will spend her ill-gotten gains. Dwelling on the thought of a long vacation in some idyllic holiday destination, she even permits herself a very faint smile of contentment.

Chapter 55

Paul is desperate to leave the stifling courtroom to return home to Rita for some mutual comforting and reassurance. Rita has remained absent from her employment during the trial. Quite simply she would not be capable of disguising that she is deeply troubled in a work situation. However, every day has dragged by so very slowly and her energy levels are positively sloth-like.

Paul duly arrives home from court and is warmly greeted by Rita's tear-stained but smiling face. She has just spent a couple of hours in Emma's bedroom looking at all her little girly effects and smelling them to remind her of her little daughter. She is desperate to hear how the trial has been going.

'Please, please tell me there is some good news.'

'Well, it's not bad news,' says Paul. 'At the moment, we have a hung jury with the slight majority in our favour,' he says, trying to put a positive slant on it. 'So it is just up to me to influence the others to vote not guilty. The good news is that we do not need to persuade everyone to vote our way. The judge has said that a ten to two majority will suffice. This is just as well given that the foreman seems very determined to convict.'

The Websters endure a terrible night's sleep. They are wrapped so tightly in each other's arms, as if they might lose another loved one if they were to let go. Daylight is welcomed, but what will the new day have in store for the Websters?

Chapter 56

The following morning, all the jurors return to court before formally being invited to continue their deliberations in the jury room. Following the vote for the role of foreperson, it is now Albert Patterson who has the benefit of the talking stick.

'Good morning all, I hope everyone has had a good night's sleep. Equally, I hope that, as instructed, you did not discuss the case with anyone, including family. You will recall that yesterday, to use boxing parlance, we had a split decision. Equally, as you know, there are a number among you who are as yet undecided.

'The purpose of today is to try to influence those who are undecided to vote one way or another with a view to securing a sufficient majority, if not a unanimous vote. Please note that members of the jury are of course fully entitled to change their vote at any stage of the process.

'Before starting today, perhaps we should have another show of hands, lest there has been any change of heart. Those voting guilty?'

Five hands are raised.

'Those voting not guilty?

Four other hands are raised.

'And those undecided?'

The remaining three jurors raise their hands. The pendulum has swung very slightly in favour of a guilty vote. It is unlikely that anyone else in the juror's room will have noticed the completely forlorn look on the face of Paul Webster. Our foreperson once again takes control of the situation.

'Clearly, a few of us will require to be persuaded if we are to come to a conclusion that is satisfactory to the court. Accordingly, I will now disclose the factors which, to my mind, clearly point towards guilt on the part of the accused, and then I will invite Paul Webster to make the opposing arguments as we are obviously in different camps. In the meantime, should anyone have any queries, please don't hesitate to ask. Equally, should you have any questions of the judge, please feel free to use me as a conduit.

'Ok, so let's begin. Firstly, let me say that I feel there is an avalanche of evidence pointing towards Miles Lamont being the guilty party. In the interests of note-taking, I have numbered the various points that have brought me to my decision. Apologies if they are not in chronological order:

One – Has there been the slightest suggestion that someone else might have assaulted the victim? "No" is the answer to this question. Even the defence counsel has not suggested so.

Two – The accused was seen by two or three independent witnesses at the scene of the crime in or about the time the attack took place.

Three – The accused had the victim's blood on his clothing.

Four – The accused tried to hide his bloodstained item of clothing.

Five – If the accused was attacked by the victim, why did his clothing not show any evidence of his own blood? Nor have we been provided with any images of bruising on the accused's person.

Six – The accused was under the influence of drink and possibly drugs on the night in question. The victim was not.

Seven – The accused was much younger, fitter and more robust than the victim.

Eight – What motive could the victim possibly have for attacking the accused, as the defence would have you believe?

Nine – By contrast, the accused whilst intoxicated was angry because he was not being given access to more beer.

Ten – Finally, there was the sighting of him at the station close to the public phone box having already abandoned Harinder Singh to his fate.

Eleven – We heard from Gerry Smith at the end of the prosecution evidence that there was a previous incident when the accused had reverted to violence – proof that he has a violent disposition.

In my view, the evidence against the accused is quite overwhelming. However, let me now pass you over to Paul to advance the case for a not guilty verdict.'

'Thank you Albert. I would ask you all to try to remember the charge to the jury by Russell Holstein for the defence. He emphasised that nobody witnessed any assault taking place. Strictly speaking, that is nobody except perhaps for Johnny Morgan. I accept that we might not regard him as being a very solid witness. However, it would appear that he is the only one who can shed any light on what actually took place that fateful evening. If you are to believe Morgan's evidence, then Lamont was not the aggressor.'

'Yes, there are bits and pieces of circumstantial evidence that have been put before us, with the accent on the word "circumstantial". If any of you feel absolutely positive in your own mind that Miles Lamont is guilty, then I would invite you to place your vote accordingly. However, should you feel having heard all the evidence that he possibly, or even probably, committed the crime, then you must vote with me – not guilty. Quite simply, "possibly" or "probably" is just not good enough.'

'Finally, I would task each and every one of you to remember the end of the address by Russell Holstein for the defence. He suggested if it were your son in the dock, or any other close young family relative, how would you feel about them being sent away, possibly for life, on the basis that "he possibly or probably did it?' You will recall that it has to be proved beyond a reasonable doubt that he committed the crime. Is there anyone here who can put their hand on their heart and say that they do not have a reasonable doubt?'

Discussions follow for several hours with disagreements and arguments aplenty, during which Paul Webster tries to use all his powers of persuasion. At one stage, the only common denominator is that they do not want to be stuck in the jury room for another day as they are all desirous of arriving at a conclusion.

Chapter 57

Like a virus, word has spread very rapidly throughout the court and the immediate vicinity that the jury has eventually reached a verdict and they will be returning to court before long. There is a scurry of activity within the media. Constance and Felicity gulp down their coffees and apply more lipstick in nervous anticipation.

TV crews are setting up outside the court hoping to catch some coverage of the accused in jubilant mood, if found not guilty. Alternatively, they will be on hand to snap his anguished family members in the event that the result does not go his way. Equally inside the court, members of the press are juggling for position. There is suddenly a real buzz of anticipation in the air. The public areas are rapidly filling up with the various factions naturally migrating to those seating areas they have been occupying each day. Some have even chosen to leave a garment or two on seats in order to mark their territory. 'Towels and sun loungers' are brought to mind. The only departure from this is Constance and Felicity who tend to sit wherever they are most visible to the cameras. In the press area, they spot Mike Walsh, the reporter, and then immediately look away.

In another area are Derek, Olivia and Mel Lamont with close family and friends. Then, occupying a separate part of the courtroom are Meeta, Charanjeet and Aasha Singh plus friends and family. In addition, there are members of the Sikh community adding a splash of colour to the proceedings with their white, blue, yellow and orange turbans. There is one lower profile but highly significant group of people who are scattered about the courtroom and all of whom have their own very special interest in the outcome of proceedings. This group includes Johnny Morgan, DI Jean Ronald, Kenny Freeman and Andy Winters. Of course, there are also members of the general public, some of whom are regulars who look on court as a means of fulfilling their soap opera fix. The remainder are merely tourists wishing to tick the Old Bailey off their attraction list.

Once everyone else is assembled, the jury are called back into court. They look absolutely shattered after hours of deliberations. As the noise levels in the public benches rise, the clerk of court calls for silence before bowing to the judge. He then invites the accused to rise before turning to address the jury.

'Members of the jury, would your foreperson please stand?'

Albert Patterson proudly rises with a folded piece of paper in hand.

'Has the jury reached a verdict on which you are all agreed?'

'No,' answers the foreperson in a loud and clear voice. At this point, one could almost touch the tension in the air.

'Has the jury reached a verdict upon which at least ten of you are agreed?'

'Yes, we have.' The foreperson very slowly and ceremoniously opens the sheet of paper, looks towards Judge Templeton and reads from it. 'We find the defendant, Miles Lamont, to be not guilty of the charge of murder.'

Suddenly the court is in an uproar. Paul Webster obviously already knew the result, but hearing it said out loud provides the necessary affirmation that is so important to him. Given the sense of relief on his face, any observant onlooker might be forgiven for thinking that he is related to the accused.

Derek, Rita and Mel Lamont indulge in a threesome cuddle as they all jump about as one. The Singhs stand in silence, staring straight ahead in disbelief, obviously inclined to the view that the criminal justice system has betrayed them. Constance and Felicity jump and cheer and immediately herald the need for a celebration party.

Meanwhile, Andy Winters permits himself a little self-indulgent smile for a job well done. The very instant the verdict is announced and before the jury is formally discharged, he rushes out of the courtroom – a man on a mission. Meanwhile, the accused punches the air several times in a triumphant salute, but yet fails to acknowledge the sterling efforts on behalf of Walter Bryson and Russell Holstein, his successful defence team. The judge then has a few last words for the jury.

'Ladies and gentlemen, the trial is now at an end and I thank you all for your service. You have carried out a most important role in our society and I am most grateful to you for your time and attention. I am pleased to say that you are now released from all your obligations. It is often the case at the end of a jury trial that counsel for the prosecution or for the Crown would like a word with the jurors to enquire of you as to what influenced you in your final decision. You are not obliged to do so, but it can prove to be very helpful to them. You are all now excused, thanks once again.'

He also thanks counsel and their legal teams before advising Miles Lamont that he is a free man. At this point, Miles looks for Chas Singh in the public gallery and leers at him for almost thirty long seconds. His facial expression is one that Chas will never, ever forget.

Chapter 58

Paul Webster quickly makes his way through a myriad of press representatives while exiting the Old Bailey. He is gaunt and cadaverous in appearance resulting from an accumulation of long sleepless nights, coupled with a loss of appetite. Despite his grave situation, he still manages a smirk. If only the press knew that the killer of all killer stories is at that very moment just walking right under their noses and out of the courtroom. But their sights lie on another much more obvious prize. In the meantime, Paul is a man with mixed emotions. While the court judgement has been favourable to his cause, his estranged daughter is still not yet back in the fold.

Paul phones Rita to share the good news with her but is desperately keen to go home to hopefully hear again from his daughter's abductors. He does not have long to wait. As he opens the front door, he sees the now familiar envelope, 'ABOUT EMMA'. His first thought is why Rita has once again not heard the letterbox opening or closing. Rita rushes to meet him and he cannot help but notice her red-rimmed eyes encircled in black shadows. The abduction of their precious daughter is certainly starting to take its toll.

She slows down as she notices the envelope in Paul's hand.

Without any words passing between them, they make their way to the lounge for a ceremonial opening:

> WELL DONE PAUL. YOU MUST HAVE BEEN VERY PERSUASIVE IN THE JURY ROOM! I TOLD YOU ALREADY THAT I KEEP MY WORD AND SO YOUR LOVELY DAUGHTER EMMA WILL BE RETURNED TO YOU UNHARMED THIS EVENING. HOWEVER, IF THERE IS ANY SIGN OF THE POLICE AT THE HANDOVER, OR IF I FIND THAT I AM BEING FOLLOWED, THEN EMMA WILL DIE. PAUL, YOU MUST REMAIN AT HOME UNTIL YOUR DAUGHTER IS RETURNED. IF YOU LEAVE THE HOUSE THIS EVENING, EMMA WILL DIE. IF YOU TELEPHONE THE POLICE, I WILL KNOW AND EMMA WILL DIE.
>
> IF YOU FOLLOW MY INSTRUCTIONS TO THE LETTER, EMMA WILL BE BACK SLEEPING IN HER OWN BED THIS EVENING – HER LIFE IS ENTIRELY IN YOUR HANDS.
>
> RITA, I WANT YOU TO DRIVE (ON YOUR OWN) TO MARKET STREET. GO TO THE DISUSED BUS STOP OPPOSITE THE OLD POST OFFICE AND BE THERE AT EXACTLY 7.00 PM. WHEN THERE, YOU WILL BE CONTACTED ONCE AGAIN. SOMEONE WILL BE WATCHING YOU EVERY STEP OF THE WAY. LEAVE YOUR MOBILE PHONE AT HOME. WHEN YOU PARK YOUR CAR IN MARKET STREET, LEAVE IT UNLOCKED. IF WE FIND A MOBILE PHONE ON YOUR PERSON OR HIDDEN SOMEWHERE IN YOUR CAR, THEN EMMA WILL DIE.
>
> YOUR DAUGHTER IS NOW ALMOST WITHIN TOUCHING DISTANCE – DO NOT BLOW IT NOW!

Paul and Rita cuddle and cry, and cuddle and cry. In the meantime, Millie their beloved cockapoo, sits looking up at them, moving her head from side to side with that expression of puzzlement or bewilderment that some dogs are so truly expert at creating.

Suffice to say that neither Paul nor Rita have ever even entertained the idea of contacting the police – quite simply, the stakes have always been way too high.

Chapter 59

Before having even left the sanctity of the court building, Derek Lamont declares to all within earshot that they are invited to a party at their house that very evening. As well as family and friends, he invites Russell Holstein who very promptly, but politely, declines. Also asked is Walter Bryson and, of course, no party would be complete without Olivia's friends, Constance and Felicity.

By contrast, the Singh family are totally devastated with the result of the trial. They had closed their corner shop during the trial, but now out of financial necessity they need to be fully operational again very quickly.

Johnny Morgan, whilst also invited to the celebration party, has declined on two fronts. Firstly, he is not in a party mood given that a potential perjury charge is still looming over his head. Besides that, simply being in the company of Miles has proved not to be good for one's wellbeing.

As far as Russell Holstein is concerned, he is just delighted to have yet another notch on his barrister belt. He is fast becoming a silk of considerable experience and renown. By contrast, Joan Calvert makes her weary way back to chambers to catch up on all the emails that have dropped into her inbox whilst at trial. Better days certainly lie ahead for her.

As for Judge Templeton, the golf course beckons.

DI Jean Ronald genuinely feels sorry for her Detective Constables. What a shame after all their earnest endeavours. She invites them along to the local pub as a way of winding down and also as an opportunity to boost their dented confidence. Tomorrow will bring a new day, new criminals and new challenges. So the three of them wander off to their local and Jean Ronald gets the drinks in. They make a pact not to discuss the case. The first drinks slip down a treat as do the second and third. They are enjoying letting off some steam after the stress of having to provide evidence. However after the third drink, Janet Green has to excuse herself as she has arranged to go to the cinema with her partner.

'One for the road?' asks Jean of Andrew.

'It would be rude to refuse,' says Andrew with a smile.

A rather cute smile, thinks Jean to herself as the wine is starting to take effect. She has always found Andrew to be attractive, but given that she is his superior, has never looked at him in a romantic kind of way. On a couple of occasions, their hands touch, but is it by accident or design? There is certainly some chemistry developing between them judging by their mutual body language.

'Another one for the road,' says Andrew with a glint in his eye.

'Would be rude to refuse,' she replies, echoing his earlier response.

By this time, they are both feeling a bit woozy and extremely relaxed in one another's company. There now almost appears to be a realisation between them that their relationship has moved on to a new level. Andrew leans forward to kiss Jean and there is no resistance – au contraire! Okay, their 'dalliance' might be partly fuelled by alcohol, but nevertheless, there is an intensity, warmth and closeness which suggests that this might just be something a little special. At the end of the evening, Jean invites Andrew back to her house and he duly agrees. In fact, he overnights. They share stories, feelings, a bed and a toothbrush. They have reached the point of no-return as far as their working relationship is concerned.

Chapter 60

Agonisingly, the Websters sit watching the clock on the wall in the vain hope that it might magically make it move faster. Openly they are both so, so excited about Emma's impending return, but privately each of them harbour their own thoughts – quite dark, unspeakable thoughts. Although Emma's abductor said that they were a person of their word, that is really all they have to cling on to, and cling on they do.

At long last, it is now time for Rita to leave. She is experiencing a cocktail of emotions. She is quivering with fear but at the same time nurturing warm feelings of anticipation, anticipation of seeing her beloved daughter. Paul is to stay at home as directed, but this time around, arguably his role is the more agonising one, especially since Rita cannot remain in telephone contact.

Rita grips the steering wheel so tightly she has indentation marks on the palms of her hands. She notices a police patrol car coming in the opposite direction and immediately feels sick in her stomach. She and Paul have already decided that she should drive at a very sedate pace to ensure she does not invite any unwanted police attention. She glances in her interior mirror and watches it disappear in the distance. Breathing a deep sigh of relief, she then continues on her journey, driving even more conservatively than before.

It is 6.55 pm when Rita arrives at Market Street. As per instructions, she parks up the car and leaves it unlocked before walking to the disused bus stop. She stands there for what seems like an eternity but is actually a mere five minutes. This used to be a relatively bustling area, but when the post office closed, it sadly had a domino effect on other local commercial and retail outlets. Suddenly, the eerie silence is broken with the ring call of a mobile phone which she realises is located in the waste bin attached to the old bus stop pole. She swiftly retrieves it and answers.

'Hello'?

'Hi Rita,' says a man's voice. 'We are currently watching you and your husband, and so far you have done very well. Let's keep it that way, shall we?'

'Yes, but please, please don't hurt our little girl.'

'We won't, provided you play ball.'

'We've done everything you've asked.'

'Just keep it that way and all will be fine. Also, these are both burner phones we are using, so no point in passing yours to the police or anyone else – and in any event, it has also been wiped for prints.'

Nervously, Rita responds. 'Don't worry, I will do anything you ask to get my daughter back.'

'Ok. Start walking in the direction of the town centre and stay connected to me on the phone at all times.'

There is silence for a while and Rita finds this to be extremely disarming. Eventually, further instructions come through.

'Turn first left at the church and then first right. Remember, we are watching you at all times.'

Then there is another prolonged silence during which time Rita is shaking with fear and apprehension. Then the mobile rings again.

'Take the next street on the left and you will see a children's playground on your right. Walk straight towards it.'

Chapter 61

Carol Winters does not attract any undue attention or unusual glances as she walks hand in hand with Emma. To any casual observer, she is just a normal mum walking with her daughter towards the local play park. They are swinging arms and Emma is very happy having been told that she is about to meet her mummy.

Upon arrival at the play park, Carol allows Emma to enjoy the merry-go-round, the see-saw and the chute in the company of her new best pal, Eddie the Teddy. Last of all are the swings.

'Ok,' says Carol, 'would you like to see your mum now?' The answer is not in doubt. 'Ok, I promise that if you sit on the swing, close your eyes really tight and count very, very slowly to one hundred, then your mum will be in front of you to give you loads of kisses and hugs. But if you count too quickly or if you open your eyes even a tiny little bit, you will not see your mum. Do you understand?'

'Yes,' says Emma with her eyes so tightly screwed together her face is all crunched up.

She has just counted to eighty-eight when she hears her mum scream out her name from a distance at the very top of her voice. She is so excited but still keeps counting with her eyes closed until she is completely smothered with hugs and kisses. Carol Winters watches the happy reunion from a distant hill.

'Emma, we love you so, so, so much,' says Rita, who then has a complete emotional breakdown. Eventually, she gathers herself and walks back towards her car with her. She holds Emma so very tight. She never wants to let go of her ever again. Emma insists in introducing her mum to Eddie.

Chapter 62

For the Singh family, life will never return to normal after the loss of their patriarch. However, Harry's Corner Store is doing great business and Chas is being groomed by his mum to eventually take over the running of it. He has already introduced a few more potential income streams, such as the selling of lottery tickets which has considerably enhanced footfall to the shop. It will always be Harry's name above the door, but the operation may have a slightly more modern twist. Aasha's medical studies are going well, but what a terrible shame that Harinder did not live to see his only daughter become a doctor.

As for the Lamonts, nothing much has changed. Derek, notwithstanding having paid a quite exorbitant cash sum to Walter Bryson, is doing okay financially by continuing to accumulate a small fortune through his drug dealings. He is also still turning a blind eye to his son dabbling in drugs. In his eyes, Miles is a rising star in the business and is still capable of doing no wrong. Olivia continues to do her utmost to spend money like it grows on trees. In the meantime, thanks to Dad, Mel now has her own little hairdresser's business on Westwood Main Street. Yes, 'Hair by Mel' is thriving.

The Websters are trying, as best they possibly can, to live a normal life. However, quite understandably they are more possessive than ever over Emma. As recommended by their GP, they are undergoing trauma counselling and have even contemplated some treatment for little Emma who returned to school a couple of weeks after the trial. Millie, the cockapoo – and no doubt Daisy as well – seem delighted that their friend Emma is back home to play with them.

Nothing new to report with Constance and Felicity. They are both bordering on being professional socialites, still hanging on to the coattails of Olivia.

Detective Inspector Jean Ronald is now firmly entrenched in a major robbery case that has taken place in the city. She continues to be identified by her superiors as being a rising star. Meanwhile, her two Detective Constables continue to impress with the level of their endeavours. DI Jean Ronald and DC Andrew Gordon are having clandestine meetings a couple of evenings per week. However, while in the workplace they are trying, with difficulty, to restrict themselves to the occasional knowing or loving look.

The career of Joan Calvert is still on a steady upward path despite the reversal in the Lamont case. Russell Holstein's reputation as an achiever at the bar has been done no harm whatsoever by this result and he finds himself in constant demand by instructing solicitors.

Johnny Morgan is still keeping a low profile. He lives in hope that the police don't come knocking at his door or that he receives a court summons through the post.

Walter Bryson has had a windfall thanks to the Lamonts, and he has booked a round-the-world cruise for him and his wife. He has also treated himself to a new Porsche sports car.

Andy and Carol Winters are also living off the proceeds of their latest dodgy deal and are eagerly seeking out their next one.

Chapter 63

Emma's teacher, Miss Anne Richardson, is becoming repeatedly concerned about Emma's behaviour in class. She is being increasingly withdrawn and distant. In addition, she has been spotted on occasions crying and has also wet her pants once or twice – all completely out of character. Eventually one lunchtime, Miss Richardson decides to stay behind for a little chat with her. She mentions to Emma that she will be back in a few moments as she wants to also involve the Head Teacher, Maureen Higgins. As she closes the classroom door behind her, she hears an almighty, bloodcurdling scream from within, followed by a heartrending plea.

'No, please, please don't lock me in,' Emma cries, followed by some frantic sobbing.

Miss Richardson rushes back in, puts her arm around Emma and comforts her, reassuring her that she is not going to lock the door. Emma eventually calms down. Five minutes or so later, they then walk together to the head teacher's office.

Befitting her position, Mrs Higgins displays an excellent bedside manner and places herself at Emma's level, both physically and mentally.

'What is upsetting you, Emma? Miss Richardson tells me that

you have not been your usual self lately?' This is met with silence. 'Why were you thinking you might be locked in the classroom?'

Emma starts to sob again, but through her tears, she asks the most innocent of questions. 'If I am asked to keep a secret, does that mean I can't even tell my teacher?'

'Emma darling, of course you can trust your teachers. Both of us just want to help you and make you happy again.' The teachers are not at all expecting the response they receive.

'I was locked up in a bedroom for a few days and not allowed out except when I was taken to the toilet.' Miss Richardson and Mrs Higgins are temporarily speechless.

'By your parents?' asks Miss Richardson.

'No, by a woman called Sarah.'

'Who is Sarah?'

'I don't know, I had never seen her before.'

Both teachers struggle to disguise their utter surprise at what they have just heard. Emma is not prone to storytelling and there is every reason to believe there is at least an element of truth to what she is saying.

#

'Hello, Mrs Webster, it is Mrs Higgins, the head teacher at Emma's school. Don't worry, she has not had an accident or anything of that kind, but before you pick her up today, could you maybe pop in to see me for a chat, say at three o'clock? We will arrange for one of the other teachers to sit with Emma while we are chatting.'

'Of course,' says Rita, somewhat caught by surprise.

Three o'clock duly arrives as does Rita Webster. Mrs Higgins ushers her into her room. Miss Richardson is also in attendance.

'Thanks for coming in at such short notice, Mrs Webster. I will come straight to the point. We are somewhat concerned about Emma, or rather about something she has revealed to us. It is all the more worrying as I am told by Miss Richardson that, unlike one or two of her classmates, she is a child who is not inclined towards wild imaginings.'

Mrs Higgins then relays the account given by young Emma regarding her abduction. Mrs Webster's facial expression does not display any surprise or bewilderment but rather one of total resignation, perhaps even bordering on relief. She then has a total breakdown. Between sniffles and sobs, she relays the whole story of her husband being on jury duty, her daughter being abducted and the ongoing threats to her daughter's life.

'If it had been your daughter, would you not have done the same?'

Mrs Higgins somewhat diplomatically chooses not to respond to this very specific question. Rather, she looks at her in a very benign, sympathetic and understanding manner before giving her a warm embrace. Every picture tells a story.

'Mrs Webster, believe me, I have every sympathy for your situation and cannot imagine what you and your husband have gone through. I truly mean that. But equally, you will understand that I would not be doing my duty as headmistress if I were not to report this matter to the police. Indeed, I have absolutely no option.'

By this point, Rita Webster is fully resigned to her fate. In fact, she even feels a burden has been lifted off her shoulders. Rightly or wrongly, her major concern at this stage is what her husband's reaction might be given that they had made a pact to remain silent.

Chapter 64

Jean Ronald is extremely surprised to receive a call completely out of the blue.

'Detective Inspector Ronald, my name is Mrs Maureen Higgins, the head teacher at Westwood Primary School. I have a very serious matter I would wish to discuss with you. I understand that you were in charge of a recent murder inquiry where the accused was a certain Miles Lamont?'

'Yes, that is correct.'

'Well, it appears that I have some evidence of jury tampering. More specifically, a child of one of the jurors was abducted with a view to influencing the final jury verdict. This came to light because the child in question, six-year-old Emma Webster, was showing signs of emotional trauma while at school having allegedly been locked in a room for several days. Eventually, once a verdict of not guilty was returned, the child was re-united with her parents, unharmed – well at least physically. Had the Websters not carried out the instructions to the letter, the abductors threatened on a few occasions to murder their daughter. The name of the juror in question, Emma's natural father, is Paul Webster. Having asked Emma's mum in to discuss her daughter's out-of-character behaviour, she eventually broke down and relayed the whole story to us. I made Mrs Webster aware that I was left with no alternative but to bring this to your attention. She fully understood and in fact I had the distinct impression that she was to some extent relieved to have been able to share her terrible burden with someone. In short, the Websters will be anticipating hearing from you.'

'Mrs Higgins, we thank you for bringing this matter to our attention. We are most grateful, and you may rest assured that we will take matters from here. In the first instance, we will naturally be making contact with Mr and Mrs Webster. We may also wish to speak further with you at some point.'

That very evening, DI Ronald arranges to meet with the Websters at their house. As far as the Websters are concerned, there is no point in hiding anything following Emma's revelation and so they provide full disclosure. Absolutely nothing is concealed and they also hand over the threatening notes they had received. Unfortunately, there are not any external CCTV cameras at the Webster's house, but Jean Ronald makes a mental note to have one of their team check with their neighbours.

Paul Webster also speaks in detail about his jury experience and how he had to use every last ounce of his persuasive powers in order to affect the verdict of the jury. DI Ronald cannot help but feel some sympathy for the plight of the Websters and inwardly questions herself as to how she would have reacted had she been in the same circumstances.

The following day, arrangements are made for an Achieving Best Evidence Interview (ABE) with a specialist detective to 'chat' with young Emma in the presence of an appropriate adult. Unfortunately, Emma is too young to provide a worthwhile description of her abductor, known to her as Sarah.

'She has darkish hair and just looks like a mum.' Nor can she describe anything in the bare-walled bedroom that would provide any clue to her captor's identity. However, when asked specifically about the bathroom, she did notice a man's shaving equipment, suggesting that the abductor had a partner – presumably her partner in crime. In addition it was a male voice on the phone directing Rita to the play park.

Following this, Jean Ronald then telephones the Director of the

Crown Prosecution Service, a William Barnes, to advise him of this important development and more specifically the fact that there has been a clear case of witness tampering. They are agreed that under current legislation, the High Court is enabled to make an order quashing an acquittal in circumstances where the acquittal results from interference with, or intimidation of, a juror or witness. In such circumstances, an acquitted person can be re-tried for the original offence.

In the meantime, DC Janet Green has been tasked with checking with neighbours of the Websters. Fortunately, one neighbour, Mrs Edith Parker, had noticed a man putting something through the Webster's letterbox on a couple of occasions. She particularly noticed him on two counts. Firstly, she thought his appearance – tracksuit bottoms, dark hoodie and trainers – coupled with his general demeanour made him look a fraction undesirable and not in keeping with the area. Secondly, she had continued to watch him to check if he was distributing flyers to all the houses and that she might also be in receipt of one. DC Green surmises there was also a third reason – she was basically nosey. In any event, Mrs Parker thinks she would be able to recognise him again and is invited down to the police station to look at some photos of known criminals operating in the area. She seems overly delighted to have been asked.

Chapter 65

DI Jean Ronald has difficulty thinking of anything else apart from the Harinder Singh case following the call from Mrs Higgins. In addition, she has always felt that she had some unfinished business with the witness, Johnny Lamont. She is firmly of the view that he was clearly untrustworthy whilst giving evidence in the witness box. For this reason, she decides to pay him another visit. On this occasion, she has the blessing from the Crown Prosecution Service to offer him a deal in return for a comprehensive, honest and forthright statement of what actually happened on the evening Harinder Singh was killed, assuming it results in a conviction. In return, the Crown will not charge him with perjury; he will be a free man no longer having this hanging over his head. It is pointed out to him that any such conviction would forever be on his record and would undoubtedly be a hindrance in his future career, with a university degree or otherwise.

Even DI Ronald is in awe at how quickly Johnny capitulates. Obviously, the whole situation has been preying on his mind for so long and coming clean now is in some way lifting a great weight from his shoulders. He spouts forth exactly what happened that fateful night as well as going into detail about the attack and threat from Balaclava Man. Unfortunately however, he is understandably unable to give any description of his attacker save to say that he was physically strong and spoke with a local accent. From her years of experience of assessing witnesses, DI Jean Ronald just knows that this time around she is hearing the one true version of events, albeit his third! She is now dealing with intimidation of a witness and a juror – the plot is thickening and perhaps, just perhaps, the net is closing.

Chapter 66

DI Ronald has arranged a meeting with William Barnes, Director of Prosecutions. Also present is Joan Calvert who has retained a very personal interest in the case. DI Ronald provides a general background before going into more detail about the intimidation which has taken place.

'Firstly, we have a situation where there was extreme threatening behaviour towards a crucial prosecution witness by the name of Johnny Morgan. He was physically attacked by a masked assailant who claimed that he knew where his parents lived and worked and that they would be subjected to violence if he gave evidence against Miles Lamont or if he contacted the police. As a result, Mr Morgan lied under oath in order to protect his parents. As you are aware, we recently offered him the opportunity to avoid prosecution himself in return for full disclosure and he has co-operated to the fullest possible extent.

'In this case, the criminals have gone for a belt and braces approach in that they have also been guilty of jury tampering. On the first day of the trial, they abducted a six-year-old child, the daughter and only child of Paul and Rita Webster. On several occasions, they threatened to kill the child, Emma, unless Mr Webster managed to persuade his fellow jurors to find Miles Lamont not guilty – the verdict which was ultimately returned. The child has now been safely returned to her parents, but I can only surmise what pain and extreme anguish they have endured.' DI Ronald then continues. 'We are of course prioritising the apprehension of the guilty party or parties and will keep you updated as to progress.'

Chapter 67

DI Ronald has called another meeting with DC Green and DC Gordon. Having ensured they are both fully updated with regard to events, she then discusses tactics going forward.

'I think it is a fair assumption that the party or parties involved in the abduction, and those involved in the witness intimidation, are one and the same. Also, we could well be dealing with a couple as a woman was involved in the abduction and a man featured in the assault. We are going to attack this on various fronts.

'One – We have the evidence of Mrs Edith Parker who spotted a man putting a note through the Webster letterbox. She has been invited down to the police station to look at some mugshots. If unsuccessful, perhaps we could use her assistance to create an artist's impression. Andrew, I will allocate this task to you.'

'Two – Paul Webster was told, rightly or wrongly, that he was being watched at all times. I would not be at all surprised if the abductor was present at court. I would like you to scan the public benches on CCTV and also outside the courtroom to check if there is anyone who might be of particular interest to us. In the first instance, I would be inclined to concentrate on the day in which Johnny Morgan was giving his evidence. This could be a very lengthy process, so perhaps you could split this task between you.'

'Three – Janet, I would ask you to have a chat with Emma's parents. Ask them if Emma can recall what her abductor was wearing when she took her to the play park?'

'Four – I would imagine that the people we are looking for are not at the top of the criminal tree. Rather, they are most probably the "hired helps", albeit fairly expensive ones. This brings Derek Lamont to mind as he is well capable of splashing the cash. So please also look out for any communication with or knowing looks between Derek and any unknown third party. Also, please try to identify those sitting near Derek Lamont in court. I will leave this task to you, Andrew.'

'Thanks in anticipation, guys.'

Chapter 68

Arrangements have again been made for young Emma Webster to be interviewed by video by two specialist ABE detectives in the company of an appropriate adult. Emma has been re-united with her favourite doll, Daisy, and so poor Eddie the Teddy is excluded from this interview having moved one slot down the pecking order.

'Hi Emma, and is this the famous "Daisy" that I have heard so much about?' asks one of the detectives in an attempt to put her at ease.

Emma does not respond apart from pulling Daisy even closer, very obviously acting as her comfort blanket.

'Yes, that's right, and I've introduced him to Daisy.'

'Emma, I just wondered if you can remember anything else about the house that you lived in with Sarah? I believe that's where you met Eddie the Teddy?'

'What did you do when you were in Eddie's house?'

'I just played with toys and watched cartoons, but it became boring.'

'And what about meals, did you leave your bedroom for them?'

'No, they were brought in to me by Sarah. Sometimes I got spaghetti hoops and once I even got ice cream.'

'Did you ever leave the bedroom?'

'Only when I said I needed the toilet and I was taken there and back.'

'Was it only Sarah in the house?'

'During the day, there was only Sarah, but I thought I could hear her speaking to a man some evenings.'

'Did you hear what was said?'

'No, it was too far away. The only time I could hear her was when she was on the phone in the hall.'

'What did you hear her say?'

'I cannot remember what was said, but I heard her saying "Andy" a few times.'

At this point, one of the detectives leans forward in his seat and even young Emma must have realised that she might just have hit the jackpot.

'Emma, are you absolutely sure the name was Andy?'

'Yes,' says Emma.

'Just a couple more questions for now, Emma. You are doing really well. I believe that Sarah walked with you to the play park. Did you ever see the outside of the house where you were staying?'

'No, when I was taken there and when I left it, my eyes were always closed or covered.'

'Okay Emma, Sarah walked with you from the house to the play park. If we were to take you back to the play park, do you think that you could find the street where the house is where you were staying?'

'No, there were too many twists and turns.'

'You're doing well, Emma. I just have one last question for you. This is really important – can you remember what Sarah was wearing when she took you to the park?'

In response, Emma puts her index finger to her chin in a child-like 'now let me think' kind of pose. The detectives remain silent in case they disturb Emma's thought patterns.

'Yes, I do, she was wearing jeans and a pink tee shirt.'

'Very well done you! When you grow up, you could be a police detective.'

Emma shares a self-satisfied smile and turns to Daisy, saying, 'And you can be my assistant.'

Chapter 69

'Bingo!' announces DC Green in sheer delight. She has spent the whole morning calling on various local small businesses and also a handful of residences that are vaguely in the vicinity of the play park where Emma was re-united with her mum. She was just beginning to lose the will to live when, upon examining the CCTV from a small corner newsagent, she came across footage of a woman, probably in her thirties, wearing jeans and a pink tee shirt walking away from the general direction of the play park. DC Green is so delighted that she immediately telephones her boss to impart the good news. Arrangements are then made to use social media in the hope of securing an identification of this mystery woman.

In the meantime, DC Gordon is completely absorbed in studying CCTV of the public benches at the Old Bailey in the lookout for mugshots of any local well-known criminals.

Edith Parker has also arranged to come down to the police station as a voluntary attender. She is unable to identify the mystery man who was thought to have been putting the notes through the Websters' letterbox. This comes as no great surprise to the police given that the suspect had his hoodie up at the time – clearly not wanting to be recognised. The general consensus is that Mrs Parker has little else to keep herself busy. Her contribution is becoming questionable. Given that her description of the person is so sketchy, they incline to the view that there is no point in calling in a graphic artist. It is thought that Mrs Parker simply wants to play a part in this little drama which is unfolding.

Chapter 70

'Carol, are you at home at the moment?'

'Yes.'

'The police are on to us,' says her husband, Andy. 'Your photo has just been released by them on social media. We have so little time. Please listen very carefully to what I have to say. I need you to pack a couple of cases as quickly as possible. We will be moving and we won't be back. Put Oli in the travel holder so that he is ready to come with us. Empty out the safe taking all the cash, and don't forget our passports and anything at all of value. Remember to bring my laptop computer and your mobile. Leave your car in the driveway. In case anyone were to look in the house windows, don't leave any visible evidence that we have moved out. Once packed, take the cases through the interconnecting door to the garage, not out the front door. I will reverse into the garage and will load them from there. Do not speak to any neighbours – in fact don't speak to anyone at all, not even your mum. Speed is of the essence, darling. I will be picking you up within the hour after I attend to some other loose ends. If we do not move very quickly, we are both facing a long stretch in prison. It is important that you realise how serious this situation is. When packing, just keep in mind that we are not coming back. Also, tie your hair up, wear a baseball cap and glasses, and on this occasion, no make-up. It is paramount that you cannot be recognised.

'Oh yes, and finally, throw all the toys and dolls into a big bin bag as well as anything else from that bedroom relating to the little girl. Then wash down every surface in that room. Darling, I know you have a lot to do in a very short time, but our freedom is at stake. See you soon.'

A short time before, Andy had received a call from one of his mates saying that he had just seen Carol's photo online as being wanted in police inquiries in relation to the abduction of a young girl. Andy knew that by tomorrow at the very latest, the police would be paying them a visit. So, quick as a flash, he popped into a local travel agency, the owner of which was a personal friend. There, he paid cash for two flights from Gatwick to Malaga for the very same evening, departing at 21.20, very conveniently with the only airline that will allow very small dogs to be carried on board.

Carol is a total bag of nerves as she tries desperately to remember everything Andy had said:

...Pack two cases...

...put them in the garage...

...empty the safe...

...don't speak to anyone...

...change my appearance...

'My God, what else did he say?' The harder she tries to think, the more she panics and the more her mind blanks. 'Oh yes, wipe out any evidence of Emma having lived here – pretty crucial.'

Before too long, Carol is mightily relieved to hear Andy's car enter the driveway and then the familiar sound of the garage doors opening by remote control. No sooner has he entered the garage, than he rapidly closes the doors behind him. Sure enough there are two cases ready to be loaded together with an adjacent black bin bag. Then Carol comes running towards him giving him a massive hug as tears run down her face. With her new look – as requested – even Andy has to have a second take. Hugs over, he starts loading up the car. They then both have a quick check around the house before preparing to leave – with of course their beloved pooch, Oli, in the travel holder.

'And you remembered to check the safe, and you have all the cash?'

'Yes, Andy.'

'And passports?'

'Yes Andy.'

They first of all stop at a Cashline where they both withdraw the maximum they can on their cards. Then Andy stops at a skip where he deposits the bag of toys and dolls. Then they are on their way to the centre of town where they parked the car in a side street within walking distance of London Victoria Station before taking the Gatwick Express train.

Andy can sense Carol trembling with fear on the journey and he does all he can to calm her nerves.

'We are ahead of the game. It will probably be tomorrow before the police go looking for us, and by then, we will be sipping sangria in the sunshine. I have one or two good contacts over there, people I can trust. Also, they know people who know people, who know people. New passports, new identities, a new home and a new life for us in the sun all lies ahead of us.'

Carol seems slightly more at ease and even almost manages to smile at the prospect of fresh new beginnings. However, she cannot help shedding a tear thinking about her mum and other relations that she is leaving behind without having said her goodbyes.

'Look, Darling, everything will be fine, just try to act very casual when walking through airport security. Just imagine that we are simply going for a well-deserved fortnight's holiday in the sunshine.'

Meanwhile, poor Oli is totally oblivious to the fact that he is setting out on a new adventure.

Before long, they arrive at Gatwick Airport and the security barrier is beckoning, and suddenly Carol's confidence vanishes faster than a rat up a drainpipe. She has perhaps watched too many films or TV programmes where a member of airport security looks at a passenger, then looks on their computer followed by a 'would you please step this way, madam.'

She can hear her every step so clearly. She can also feel her heart pounding in her chest. She is all hot and bothered and imagines her face to be bright red. She has globules of perspiration running down her back. Should she look at the security person or look away? She tries to imagine what she would normally do but cannot think logically.

All her worries and concerns are unfounded as they both sail through security without incident. She takes Andy's hand into her own sweaty one and forces herself to walk and not run towards the duty free area and perceived freedom. Even having exited through security unscathed, she still has a mental picture of them receiving a tap on the shoulder accompanied by, 'Mr & Mrs Winters, not so quick if you don't mind. Please come this way!' Fortunately for them, that tap on the shoulder does not occur.

Andy has decided that rather than be in amongst the masses, they will splash out and pay for the private lounge. So within ten minutes or so, they are sitting enjoying complimentary drinks and nibbles when they hear on the nearby television: '...And if anybody knows the identity of this woman who we are looking to speak with during the course of our inquiries, then please call...' Nobody in the lounge will have noticed Carol shrink down into her chair and nudge down the skip of her baseball cap.

They then have to negotiate security at Malaga Airport. What if the British police have found their names on the flight manifest? Fortunately for them, all their fears are again completely unfounded as they walk through the security barrier untroubled.

A few hours later, they check into an airport hotel in Malaga. They both enjoy a gin and tonic before retiring for the night. However, slumbers are at a premium.

Chapter 71

'Good morning, Ma'am,' says DC Green as she takes her seat.

'Good morning, Ma'am,' echoes DC Gordon as he arrives at the door of her office skilfully balancing three mugs of coffee.

'Good morning, guys. Okay, let's get down to business,' says DI Ronald. Janet, as I recall, you had success in relation to the CCTV cameras close to the play park?'

'Yes, Ma'am. We had a strong response to our online campaign, and one woman has been named on a few occasions, namely a Mrs Carol Winters.'

'Thanks Janet.'

A video identification parade is then arranged for young Emma (accompanied by a responsible adult) to see if she can identify the woman as being 'Sarah' who kept her captive – which she does without the slightest hesitation.

'Andrew, how did you get on with the CCTV footage taken from the public benches?'

'Well, Ma'am, the trial had attracted two or three known villains. However, I was very interested to hear Janet's report. You will recall that little Emma had heard her captor talking on the phone to someone by the name of "Andy". So I was particularly interested in one known villain caught on CCTV during the trial, namely an Andy Winters.'

'Looks like we have a pair!' says DI Ronald. 'Too much of a coincidence. I suggest you both go and pay the Winters family a little social call?'

#

A few hours later

Both Detective Constables have returned to base after having visited the Winters' abode. DC Gordon immediately reports in to their boss.

'I am afraid that although there was a car in the driveway, there was nobody at home. We had a look through all the house windows and all seemed normal. That is with the exception of a room with the window boarded up to the rear of the property which we assume to be a bedroom. You may recall that Emma said her bedroom was boarded up – seems to me like one coincidence too far.'

'Thanks for that. Please arrange warrants for the arrest of both Andy and Carol Winters as well as around the clock surveillance on their house. If they do not re-appear very soon, we will request a warrant to search their house.'

Chapter 72

After a night of very restless sleep, Andy and Carol Winters wake up to their new life in the sun. However, far from sunbathing, following a healthy continental breakfast in their room, they sit down to strategise. Already, Andy, being very methodical, has made some plans for their life on the run, not wanting to leave a single item to chance. He is well aware that the police will have liaised with the airports. So while they would have no idea of their final destination, they would soon know they had flown to Malaga.

Carol is slightly shocked when her husband exits the bathroom with his head completely shaven. This will take a bit of getting used to, she thinks to herself. He has also not shaved for a couple of days with a view to growing a beard to attempt to completely transform his appearance.

He has also asked Carol, a natural brunette, to find a hairdresser and opt for a complete blonde rinse. He wishes to leave no stone unturned in their attempt to 'disappear' and create new personalities. While Carol is having her hair coloured, Andy makes plans aplenty. The first priority is to secure accommodation. However, he does not want to adopt any of the slightly more formal vehicles such as Airbnb. So he pops out to pick up an edition of the free paper read by Brits abroad entitled the 'Costa Del Sol News'. He is looking for any flats for rent on an informal cash basis where the landlord is clearly not wishing to declare the rental income for tax purposes. Eventually he chooses a one bedroom modern flat in Estepona which is modestly priced, claims to have a sea view and is within walking distance of bars and restaurants. For the moment, he has merely given his name as being Andrew with no surname offered, or asked for, and has rented it initially for a three month period. Estepona is about a twenty-five minute taxi drive from Puerto Banus and about thirty minutes from the town of Marbella.

His long-term friend and 'business associate', Harry Gibbs, runs a shady car sales showroom in Puerto Banus, a cover for his behind-the-scenes drugs business. Harry and Andy were both brought up in Bethnal Green in London's East End. Andy has jumped in a taxi and Harry is his next port of call. When he arrives, Andy makes his way past a couple of Rolls-Royces, a Ferrari and a Bentley – probably all clocked – to find Harry sitting in his back office with his feet on the desk smoking a thick Cuban cigar. A kind of likeable rogue, shades of Arthur Daley come to Andy's mind.

'My God, I don't believe it, Andy Winters. I hardly recognised you there. What happened to your hair? Have you been inside doing a stretch?'

'Good to see you, Harry, it's been quite a while. No, I've not been inside, but I am in a bit of bother with the Old Bill and need your help. Carol and I had to get out of Blighty pretty sharpish and they will be on our tail, so we need new identities.'

'What do you need?'

'New passports and driving licences for Carol and me for starters. Yes, and a Spanish dog passport for Oli.'

'These items don't come cheap these days,' says Harry.

'Whatever it takes, Harry, whatever it takes.'

'Ok, I will need a down payment of five grand.'

Andy goes into his jacket and hands over five rolls of notes.

'Well, thank you, Andy. To start the ball rolling, I will need three up-to-date passport-type photos of both you and your missus. And I think also a couple for your pooch. It should take three or four days until I have them. In the meantime, I would lie very low if I were you.'

'One more thing, Harry. We will need some wheels – nothing fancy, nothing stolen and nothing that will attract attention.'

'No probs,' says Harry, 'I will have something waiting for you when you come back for your paper work.'

Andy thanks him and then leaves feeling somewhat relieved that another pretty major box has been ticked. His next stop is to buy a couple of burner phones – a pretty straightforward task.

An hour later and Andy is back at the hotel and is greeted by someone who looks only very vaguely like his wife. Having previously had quite long dark hair, she now has cropped blonde hair and looks like a completely different person. The next priority is to check out of the hotel, have their passport photos taken, drop them in to Harry and then head to their rented accommodation. Things are moving at a bit of a pace.

Three days later, Andy and Carol Winters are no more. Following a further meeting with Harry Gibbs, they are reborn as Alan and Christine Wright, complete with new passports, Spanish driving licences and a Spanish pet passport for Oli. Also as a nod to Brexit, they are the proud owners of Spanish residency cards. In return, Harry is the recipient of wads and wads of dosh. It has been a mutually beneficial transaction.

Finally, they are given the keys to a six-year-old Spanish registered Ford Kuga. Suffice to say that both Andy and Carol are used to driving more prestigious vehicles, but this one is a perfect choice given that they wish to remain below the radar.

Chapter 73

A warrant is granted to search the house belonging to the Winters family. It has been watched around the clock and neither Mr nor Mrs Winters have returned, and so they will have to force entry. DC Gordon is tasked with the search, accompanied by two uniformed officers.

The house search is not long underway when it is discovered that the Winters couple have made a recent speedy escape. The wardrobes are almost bereft of clothes and a number of drawers have been left slightly open, indicative of a hasty departure. Also, the empty safe has been left fractionally ajar and there is no sign of any passports or other such documentation. Further confirming their suspicions is the fact that there is also no evidence of any suitcases within the house. DC Gordon telephones DI Ronald to update her on their findings. Upon hearing this, she alerts all the local airports to be on the lookout for the Winters family, blissfully unaware that she is about twelve hours too late. DI Ronald then arranges for Emma to be picked up along with her mum to visit the house belonging to the Winters. It only takes a few minutes for Emma to identify the house as being the one in which she was held captive.

Sometime later on the same day, DI Ronald is devastated to receive a call from a security official to the effect that the Andy and

Carol Winters had flown in to Malaga Airport the evening before. Yes, the net closed in but not quickly enough. She then makes contact with her Spanish counterparts, sending them photos and full details of Mr and Mrs Winters.

DI Ronald decides a discussion with Derek Lamont is well overdue, and so she arrives at his office completely unannounced. He looks unimpressed to see her and is quick to suggest that he is very busy, although this is not borne out by the dearth of paperwork on his desk. Nevertheless, DI Ronald is in no mood to be fobbed off.

'Mr Lamont, I would like to ask you a few questions and will not take up much of your time. May I ask you if the name Andy Winters means anything to you?'

'No, why should it?'

She ignores his counter question. 'How about the name Carol Winters?'

'No, never heard of her.'

'Are you quite sure?

'Yes, absolutely sure.'

Intuitively, if surprisingly, Jean Ronald thinks he is telling the truth.

'However, you do know a Johnny Morgan?'

'Yes, he is a friend of my son.'

'And did you know he was assaulted and threatened with a knife about the time the trial began?'

'No, I knew nothing about that.'

'Did you arrange for this assault to take place in order to influence Johnny Morgan's testimony in favour of your son?'

'That's total rubbish. I know nothing about any assault.'

DI Ronald is of the view that he knows more than he is saying but has made no headway, although she did secretly enjoy rattling his cage a little. When leaving his office, she passes young Miles Lamont in the corridor. She stares right at him, but he intentionally avoids her gaze.

Within minutes of her leaving his office, Derek Lamont is on the phone to Walter Bryson to tell him all about the unscheduled visit from DI Ronald. Bryson is pretty laid back in his response.

'No worries, they are only fishing, but don't you jump at the bait. Also best you don't phone me – you know where I am if you need to see me.'

Chapter 74

Several weeks have passed since the trial finished and the Lamont family are settling down to normal family life. Derek and Olivia are continuing to co-exist in their sham of a marriage. Derek is still running DL Developments as a front for his illegal drugs operation. Olivia still seems inclined to the view that regular retail therapy cures all ills. Miles, despite the promises to his maker when under threat of a long period of incarceration, continues to dabble with drugs and generally court trouble. As usual, Derek prefers to look the other way.

But for Mel, the big day has arrived, namely her twenty-first birthday, and the Lamonts don't need much of an excuse for a party. However on this occasion, they have two good reasons to celebrate as Mel has also announced her engagement to her long-term boyfriend, Stuart. The venue for the party is the Lamont abode. Derek and Olivia relish any opportunity to grandstand and showcase to others their apparent wealth. Everybody who is anybody in Westwood has been invited. And it will come as no surprise that top of Olivia's list are Constance and Felicity, the serial party-goers. Interestingly, their respective husbands are not in tow.

As well as various family members, there are also a number of Derek's business associates, all appearing to have varying degrees of legitimacy. In addition, a few neighbours have been invited to experience what the best house in the street looks like internally, even if the trappings are largely a direct result of drug dealing. The two five-foot, gold laminated elephants situated at either side of the main entrance tell their own tale!

In order to get himself in the party mood, Miles decides to pop down to the Riverview Bar in the far side of town. It is not his usual choice of hostelry. However, he had met a girl, Alice, the week before whom he strongly fancied, who said she tended to go to the Riverview at weekends. He was kind of hoping she would be there and he could invite her to his sister's party.

Miles enters the pub and has a look around, but Alice is nowhere to be seen. So he orders a pint which slips down a treat, followed by another and yet another. Despite everything that has happened to him, drink-driving is never off his agenda. His attention is then drawn to a group of young Asian guys, about five in number, who have walked into the bar. Suddenly, he realises that one of them is Chas Singh who is staring right at him. He freezes on the spot. He has just ordered and received another pint, so he does not want to leave it and walk out otherwise it will appear that he is intimidated. He concentrates on looking down into his pint glass hoping that he will not be recognised. However, from the corner of his eye, he can sense the group moving towards him.

'Well hello there, if it is not the murderer himself, Miles Lamont. Have you beaten up any old men recently for kicks?' asks Chas Singh. 'How cowardly of you to choose someone who could not defend himself. You are a coward, aren't you? Repeat after me, "I, Miles Lamont, am a coward and a murderer".'

Miles remains silent and very frightened. However, Chas is not for relenting. By this point, Miles is so wishing that his old ally Billy Blacker would come through those doors.

'Repeat after me, "I, Miles Lamont, am a coward and a murderer." What's wrong, Miles, has the cat got your tongue? Suddenly you are not so cocky now, are you?'

'I don't want any trouble.'

'I don't suppose my father did, either, but he did not have a choice.'

'I just want to finish my pint and leave,' says Miles rather meekly, if not apologetically.

'No problem,' says Chas, 'I can help you.' At that, he lifts up Miles's pint, which is still nearly full, and pours most of the contents over the Miles's head. 'I expect that will make you so angry that you will want to take me outside?'

'No, as I said, I don't want any trouble,' says Miles in a somewhat pathetic tone.

At that point, Chas and his friends "usher" Miles outside and around to the back of the pub. They stand in a circle around him, each one chanting 'murderer' in unison. They then push him from one person to another, thereby heightening his sense of humiliation.

'I am only going to give you one last chance or else this whole affair is going to get very much worse for you. Now, kneel down,' Chas shouts in a louder, angrier voice.

Shaking with fear, Miles kneels down in the middle of the circle.

'Now, repeat after me three times, "I am a coward and a murderer".'

Terrified of the potential retribution if he does not agree, Miles duly repeats the words. After each rendition, Chas makes him say it louder.

'Now, would you like to give me your car keys, after all, you should not be drinking and driving.' Miles reluctantly hands them over. 'I am merely doing my duty as a citizen by taking your keys. Now, start walking home and consider yourself very lucky you were not beaten up like my dad.'

Drenched, smelling of beer and duly chastened, Miles starts to walk the three-mile journey back to his house. When he eventually arrives thoroughly exhausted and resembling a drowned rat, it is impossible for him to access the house without being spotted by a number of the party-goers who have spilled out into the gardens. His humiliation is now complete. One might just have overheard Constance saying to Felicity, 'I told you that boy was no good. He's always been the black sheep of the family.'

Not surprisingly, Miles does not feature at the party and is not there to witness his sister's surprise birthday present from her parents. In front of all the guests, Derek ceremoniously hands her a small box which purports to be a ring box whilst encouraging everyone to sing happy birthday. The ring box actually contains a key to their garage, inside of which is a brand new white Volkswagen Beetle convertible with a large red bow tied around it. Derek secretly hopes that all assembled are suitably impressed.

Chapter 75

DI Ronald has arranged a further meeting with William Barnes, the Director of Prosecutions, for the purpose of updating him on events.

'Hi William, so much seems to have happened since we were last in touch. Let me try to bring you up to speed. We have managed to identify the couple who abducted young Emma. They are a married couple called Andy and Carol Winters. Both of them were already known to us. Andy Winters was spotted on camera at the trial. Also, his wife was identified as the abductor by the young girl, Emma. We have no evidence to suggest that Andy Winters is liable for the assault on Johnny Lamont, but we have no reason to believe that anyone else is responsible. In addition, Andy Winters does have previous for violence.'

'As you know, Johnny Morgan has revealed all to us on the basis that he will be immune from prosecution. He will provide evidence that Miles Lamont was the aggressive party and that he viciously punched and kicked his victim without reply.'

'Andy Winters is well known to the local police as a "wide boy" who seems to move from one dodgy deal to another. The not-so-good news is that the Winters couple have absconded. We are aware that they took a flight to Malaga, but where they are now is anybody's guess. We have however alerted Interpol.'

'Many thanks, DI Ronald. On the basis of all the information provided, there is justification for a retrial and I will now set the wheels in motion.'

Chapter 76

The Crown Prosecution Service is fortunate in being able to secure an early date for the retrial, namely 10 January 2022, and in due course, this is intimated to all interested parties.

Miles Lamont is now in receipt of a fresh indictment. Derek is absolutely incensed and is immediately on the phone to Walter Bryson in the vain hope that he can reverse this decision. Walter agrees to meet with him but tells Derek to manage his expectations this time around.

Joan Calvert is delighted to hear of the retrial and cancels other engagements for the week commencing 10 January as she has some unfinished business. She also looks forward to locking horns once more with Russell Holstein, but this time on a more even footing. In retrospect, she feels that at the last trial she was doing battle with one arm behind her back.

When the new date was being fixed, one of the first priorities was to ensure that Russell Holstein would be available as his intimate knowledge of the case is deemed crucial and, of course, it is in the best interests of continuity. As for Holstein himself, his natural conceit leads him to believe that he will be successful the second time around as well.

Generally speaking, the Singhs are very pleased to hear of the retrial. While it will be harrowing to listen to the evidence once more, they too have some unfinished business and they are still searching for final closure.

Absolutely crucial to the Crown case is the evidence of Johnny Morgan. Accordingly it is essential that this time around he is not 'got at'. With this in mind, the prosecution team in conjunction with the police have arranged for him and his parents to be moved to a safe house pending the trial. Fortunately his studies for the most part can be done remotely. His evidence is even more valuable second time around as he will now also be able to speak to the altercation between the accused and Gerry Smith, the doorman at Moves nightclub. As well as this, he will be able to provide corroboration of the fact that Miles was not only violent but also using and dealing in drugs – all very damning to the Crown case.

In addition, it is intended that the new jury will stay in a hotel during the length of this second trial in order to try to diminish the chance of any future jury tampering.

Needless to say that there will be no show without punch and doubtlessly Constance and Felicity will be in attendance in all their finery.

Chapter 77

Derek insists on an early appointment with Walter Bryson, and he is not going to be denied. When Derek Lamont arrives at Bryson's office, he is an angry man and nothing Bryson can say will placate him.

'Basically, on top of your normal fee, I have paid you three hundred and seventy five thousand pounds in cash to get me a result for my son – you have failed. You said that Johnny Morgan's evidence would not be a problem and that it was "sorted". Evidently this is not the case.'

'Look, Derek. I did everything you paid me to do. In my opinion, Johnny Morgan's evidence was not damning to your son's case and I also managed to get the jury on our side. What more could you expect of me?'

'I'll tell you. I would expect your little helpers to be a lot more discreet in their dealings. Had they been so, my son would not now be facing a retrial.'

'I repeat that I did–'

Derek then cuts him off. 'This time around, you will do the job properly – and I am not paying you another penny over and above your legitimate fee for representing my son and instructing counsel.'

'If you don't change your attitude, you can find another solicitor to fight your son's case,' Bryson retorts.

'No, Walter, believe me, you will represent my son, don't you worry about that. If you don't, I will notify the police that you were responsible for the attack and intimidation of a key witness and also that you were guilty of jury tampering. Not only will you be immediately struck off but you will also do a lengthy time inside. Yes, I did say, whatever it takes, but how was I ever supposed to know that you would resort to such illegal means? I would never have condoned such behaviour.'

'You lying bastard, Derek.'

'And let me give you another little incentive, Walter. If my son is ultimately found guilty, I will also be sure to reveal your dirty dealings to the police. So I suggest that you be as resourceful as possible. In short, if my son goes down, you will go down with him, shouting and screaming. Goodbye, Walter.'

As Derek storms out of his office slamming the door behind him, he leaves one very worried man in his wake.

Chapter 78

Take two! It is Monday 10 January 2022 and the retrial of Miles Lamont is about to begin. Everything seems similar to the last time around, the trial being once again held in Court Number One of the Old Bailey. The prosecution team is the same, the defence team is the same, the accused is the same, the same press representatives are present and the public benches consist of pretty much the same personnel. The one significant change is that His Honour Oscar Templeton is no longer presiding over proceedings. He has been replaced by His Honour Hector Drummond, a highly regarded and experienced judge. Also, there is a completely new jury.

The police evidence is pretty much a carbon copy of the first time around, as is the forensic evidence. The evidence of Hannah Wilson and Peter Summers is equally as robust as before.

The most significant witness is of course the one who arrives at court under police guard for his own protection, namely Johnny Morgan, who not surprisingly is somewhat nervous about giving evidence. Joan Calvert is first to take the floor.

'Is your name Johnny Morgan and are you a university student?'

'Yes, that is correct.'

'Mr Morgan, you understand why you are here today, to shed

some light on what occurred on the evening of Friday the sixth of August 2021.'

'Yes, I understand.'

Joan Calvert thinks it best to take the sting out of his testimony by immediately highlighting that Johnny had been somewhat less than honest in the past, in the hope of stealing the prosecution's thunder:

'Mr Morgan, is it also true to say that you have already given two quite different accounts as to what happened on the night in question. On the first occasion, you said to the police that you did not see any altercation between the now accused and the now deceased, Harinder Singh. Is that correct?'

'Yes.'

'And why was that?'

'Miles Lamont was a longstanding friend and he had begged me not to incriminate him, so I said that I ran off when the car stopped and that I did not see anything develop between my friend and Harry Singh.'

'So you are telling us now that this account was untrue.'

'Yes Miss, absolutely.'

'And then when this matter went to court, under oath you gave a second account. Is that again correct, Mr Morgan?'

'Yes Miss.'

'On that occasion, you gave the court a quite different account of what happened when your friend pulled up his car outside the corner shop. Is that so?'

'Yes Miss.'

'The second time around, you made the quite incredulous suggestion that after an argument Harinder Singh suddenly started beating up your friend who merely fought back in self-defence. Is that not so?'

'Yes, that's correct, that's what I said.'

'And is this account also untrue, even though on this occasion you were giving evidence under oath?'

'Yes,' responds Johnny, quite timidly.

At this point, Judge Drummond asks the witness to speak up for the benefit of the jury.

'Yes,' Johnny repeats, more forcibly.

'And why did you lie on this second occasion?' asks Joan Calvert.

Johnny hesitates and appears somewhat emotional before answering. 'I was coming home from university one evening when I was suddenly attacked by a masked man. He put a knife to my throat and I was truly terrified.' At this point, there is such a sea of murmurings emanating from the public benches that Judge Drummond has to ask for hush. 'Somehow he knew that I would be giving evidence in the trial against Miles Lamont. He also said he knew where we lived and where my parents worked. He said that if I did not say on the stand that Miles only acted in self-defence, then he would disfigure both my parents. I don't mind admitting that I was terrified and firmly believed that he would carry out his threat if I failed to do what he said.' Then looking at the jurors, he adds, 'Surely you would have done the same thing if you had been in my situation?'

At this, Russell Holstein jumps to his feet. 'Objection, My Lord, this witness should be restricted to answering questions, not asking them or dabbling in conjecture.'

'Objection sustained. Mr Morgan, please simply respond to direct questions that are put to you. Jurors, I would ask you to please disregard the last question made by this witness.'

Mrs Calvert continues her questioning. 'Mr Morgan, I understand that today under oath you are going to provide a third and quite different account of events on the evening in question. Is that correct?'

'Yes Miss'

'And to save my learned friend from asking, you originally deliberately misled the police, then under oath you lied at trial – why should anyone believe you this time around?'

'I explained why I lied the first time – to help out a friend. As for the second time around, I would lie again if I had to in order to protect my parents. I believe anyone would in my situation.'

Russell Holstein again jumps to his feet. 'Objection on the same grounds as before – speculation on behalf of the witness.'

'Objection sustained.'

'So just for the record, Mr Morgan, the account you have given today is the absolute truth?' asks Joan Calvert.

'Yes, one hundred percent.' For the very first time, Johnny has a very quick glance in the direction of the accused and is met with a steely stare.

'I would now like you to go back a little further in time.'

Judge Drummond interrupts at this point. 'Mrs Calvert, the afternoon is drawing to a close. I feel this would be an appropriate point in time to suspend proceedings as the jurors will be becoming weary.' Then turning to the jury, he says, 'Finally, I remind you not to discuss the trial with anyone except your fellow jurors. Until tomorrow.'

Chapter 79

At exactly 10.00 am, Judge Drummond takes his place on the bench ready to commence today's proceedings. The press section and the public benches are full to overflowing; the retrial has certainly caught the attention of the locals.

'I would like to recall Johnny Morgan to the stand,' says Joan Calvert. After re-taking the oath and having run through a few preliminaries. 'Mr Morgan, I would like you to cast your mind back to the week before the attack on Mr Singh. If I may be allowed by my learned friend to prompt you just a fraction, I am in fact referring to an earlier occasion when you were out with the now accused, Miles Lamont. Do you remember?'

'Yes, Miss, we went on a night out together.'

'And what did that consist of?'

'We went to two or three pubs and then went to a nightclub.'

'And how would you describe the condition of your friend that evening?'

'Objection, My Lord,' says Russell Holstein. 'This question is too general in its terms.'

Before the judge is able to make a determination, Joan Calvert counters. 'No problem, My Lord, I am very happy to be more specific.

Mr Morgan, on the night in question, was Miles Lamont under the influence of alcohol or any other substance?'

'At the beginning of the evening, I would have said that he was only under the influence of alcohol, but latterly it was a combination of alcohol and drugs.'

'Mr Morgan, please remember that you are under oath – did you partake of drugs that evening?'

'No, I did not take drugs either that night or ever in my life.'

'And did you go on anywhere after the pubs?'

'Yes, we went to a local nightclub called Moves.'

'If you don't know the answer to this question, please do not hesitate to say. Did Miles Lamont appear to be well known in this nightclub?'

'Yes, he did.'

'Is that because he is a regular?'

'Yes, I understand that he is.'

'Any other reason why he would be well known in Moves?'

Johnny Morgan hesitates before answering, and after a quick glance over to the dock, he says, 'Yes, he deals drugs in the club, or should I say he used to deal drugs in the club.'

At this, Miles puts his head in his hands. And if looks could kill, the Lamont family were killing Johnny in triplicate.

'And was he dealing drugs on the night in question?'

'Yes, but probably because he was under the influence, he was not bothering to be covert in his actions, and it came to the attention of the owner of the club and others.'

'And what followed on from that?'

'He was asked to leave the club and was banned from ever entering the premises again.'

'And did he leave the club of his own free will? 'No, he had to be escorted out by the doorman.'

'And did that go smoothly?'

'No. On the way out, he took a wild swing at the doorman, punching him in the face.'

'In summation therefore and taking a snapshot of that one evening, you experienced the now accused drinking alcohol, taking drugs, dealing in drugs and assaulting someone. Is that a fair assessment of your evidence?'

'Yes,' responds Johnny, very hesitantly.

At this point, Constance gives Felicity one of those 'what did I tell you' looks.

'Thank you, Mr Morgan, please remain on the stand as I would imagine that my learned friend may well wish to ask you a few questions.'

'Mr Holstein, over to you,' says Judge Drummond.

The Counsel for the defence does not need a second invitation. In fact, he is up and striding out towards the witness stand before Joan Calvert has even returned to her seat.

'Mr Morgan, I have listened to your very latest version of the truth with great interest – version number three, as I understand it. Are we simply supposed to guess which of the three versions, if any, is in fact the truth? If you were to return to court tomorrow, would there be a fourth version?'

Johnny Morgan simply ignores these questions. Holstein allows them to remain unanswered believing that the short impasse would have more effect on the jury. He then continues.

'Let me take you back to the night you ended up in Moves nightclub with the accused. We have already heard from you that you did not and do not take drugs. Were you drinking on that particular evening?'

'Yes, I had a couple of pints.'

'I see. At what time did you meet the accused that evening?'

'About eight p.m.'

'And at what time approximately did you go to Moves nightclub?'

'At about eleven-thirty p.m.'

'And you mentioned you were in "two or three pubs". Think carefully, Mr Morgan, was it two or three?'

'It was three.'

'And you had only two pints in three and a half hours! While all this time your pal is allegedly getting hammered. Maybe you are to be complimented for your self-discipline or self-control, or perhaps you are simply indulging in your favourite past-time, namely telling lies?'

'I said I had a few pints.'

'Did you indeed?' At this, Russell Holstein addresses the clerk of court and asks him to read out Mr Morgan's original response to the question of what he had to drink that evening.

'Yes, I had a couple of pints,' states the clerk.

Mr Holstein continues. 'In my dictionary, "a couple" means two. How long does it take you to drink a pint?'

At this point, Johnny is getting decidedly hot under the collar as he realises that he is being cornered. He is thinking to himself that he would normally consume a pint in fifteen to twenty minutes but feels it is in his best interests to extend this time frame slightly.

'About half an hour,' he retorts.

Russell Holstein allows himself a self-satisfied smile before continuing. 'So, please forgive me if my arithmetic is not quite accurate, but according to my calculation, at your own albeit subjective, self-confessed rate of drinking, you most probably had seven pints – and that is by the time you have left the last pub. And what did you have to drink in the nightclub?'

'Just one or two shots,' replies Johnny, somewhat sheepishly.

'Perhaps it would be easier if I were to use a calculator?' asks Russell Holstein, rather sarcastically. 'However, I calculate that at your regular drinking speed, you would have consumed eight or nine alcoholic drinks. Is that not so?'

'No,' replies Johnny, rather timidly.

'I am surprised that you can remember anything which happened at the nightclub. Also, it seems to me that the Crown must be a very weak case when they are relying upon an inebriated, self-confessed liar.

Joan Calvert immediately jumps to her feet. 'Objection, My Lord'.

'Sustained.'

'Finally, Mr Morgan, I would like you to satisfy my curiosity. Did my learned friend or her department make any offer to you in return for you providing us with yet another version of happenings on Friday the sixth of August 2021?'

'Yes and no.'

'What do you mean by that response, Mr Morgan?'

'Yes, I was offered something, but not for providing another version of events – for simply telling the truth.'

Joan Calvert allows herself a discreet smile, obviously impressed by his latest response.

'And what were you offered?'

'I was promised that if I now told the absolute truth, I would not be charged with perjury during the first trial, given the special circumstances of the threat to my parents.'

Russell Holstein then asks him to repeat his last answer, to ensure that all the jurors have fully taken it on board. 'Mr Morgan, is it not the case that you would say anything at all here today in order to escape being charged?'

'No.'

'Well, we shall let the jury be the judge of that, shall we? No more questions of this witness, My Lord.'

'Any re-examination, Mrs Calvert?'

'Just very briefly, My Lord. Mr Morgan, is it a fair assessment of your evidence that you initially told lies in an attempt to help your long-term friend? Then you gave a different account at trial otherwise your parents would have been very seriously harmed?'

'That is correct.'

'While I can never condone telling lies under oath, it could actually be argued that your actions were in fact driven in the first instance by loyalty to a friend and in the second, devotion to your family.'

Russell Holstein then objects again. 'I'm sorry, My Lord, but my learned friend does not appear to be asking a question, but merely stating a personal opinion.'

'Objection sustained.'

Joan Calvert then continues. 'Mr Morgan, can you look this jury straight in the eye and tell them that the account you are providing today is the truth, the whole truth and nothing but the truth?'

Looking at the jury, he very convincingly says, 'Yes.'

Chapter 80

The evidence from the other Crown witnesses follows pretty much the same lines as the original trial. Once again, the defence team strongly urges Miles Lamont not to take the stand. His parents, as guided by Russell Holstein, reinforce this viewpoint. However, Miles is being somewhat stubborn if not cocky in his attitude. He has adopted the view that if he could be found not guilty last time around without him having told his side of the story, then by him giving evidence that decision will simply be reinforced. In discussing his attitude with his parents, Holstein speaks of 'the impetuosity of youth' and confirms that sadly at the end of the day, he has to do specifically as instructed by his client.

Judge Hector Drummond decides to break for lunch after the closure of the Crown case. Russell Holstein has approximately one hour to try to persuade his client not to take the stand. There is no time to be wasted.

'Trust me, Miles, the Crown will be doing somersaults at the thought of you taking the stand. They will relish the prospect of tearing your evidence apart and also attacking your character,' said Holstein.

'But I have no previous convictions and this can be highlighted when you question me. The jury are only hearing one side of the story. I believe it to be in my best interests that they hear both sides.'

At this point, Holstein decides it is not helping his cause by continuing to try to dissuade his client from giving evidence in the short time that exists before the court reconvenes. If he were to be successful and if Miles were to be subsequently found guilty, then he would be the scapegoat. In some respects, he finds himself in a no-win situation. Yes, he will leave it up to Miles's parents to try to achieve an eleventh-hour U-turn.

The court is now in place to commence the afternoon session. Inevitably, the jurors are eager to know if the accused will be giving evidence. For the most part, they are enjoying watching the proceedings and like any good drama, do not want it to end - especially those who are experiencing a welcome escape from their mundane jobs. Those in the public benches would no doubt also like to hear from the man in the dock.

'My Lord, the defence calls to the stand the accused, Miles Lamont.'

There is a buzz of conversation and anticipation throughout the courtroom, so much so that the judge has to again call the court to order. There are the usual preliminaries: name, address, occupation and so on. Miles speaks loudly and clearly, but whether this will continue during cross-examination is yet to be seen. Russell Holstein then starts to get down to business.

'Mr Lamont, I believe you are in gainful employment?'

'Yes, I work in my father's property development company and have done so since leaving school.'

'And do you have any previous court convictions?'

'No, none.'

'Indeed, have you ever been in trouble with the police?'

'No, never.'

'Admirable' states Holstein while smiling towards the jury.

'I would like you to cast your mind back to Friday the sixth of August 2021. This was the evening that Harinder Singh was fatally assaulted. In your own words, could you please tell the court exactly what happened?'

'I decided to go on a night out and telephoned my friend, Johnny

Morgan, to see if he wanted to join me – and he agreed. So I picked him up.'

'Let me stop you there,' says Holstein. 'Were you driving the car we have had mentioned in this trial, a yellow sports BMW with a private registration, MIL5S.'

'Yes, that is correct.'

'Had you been drinking?'

'Yes, I had a beer or two before I picked up Johnny.'

'And then where did you go?'

'I stopped at Harry's corner shop to buy more beers. I know that I should not have been drinking and driving – I do hold my hands up to being guilty of that.'

'And did you get more beers?'

'No, when I stopped at the shop, the owner, Harry Singh, was just coming out. I told him that I only wanted to buy a few beers, but he locked the shop and refused to open it. I told him it would only take a couple of minutes, but he would not listen to me and simply refused to open it. I do accept that I was annoyed as I did not consider it a big ask. It is all a bit of a blur, but as I recall, I was shouting unpleasantries at him. Suddenly, he lost complete control of his temper and started attacking me. I punched back to try to defend myself and he fell. I can only assume that he must have banged his head on the ground. I panicked, jumped into my car and drove off. I should have stayed and phoned an ambulance immediately. I will forever regret not doing so.'

'May I ask, was there ever any previous bad blood between you and the now deceased? Have you had any differences of opinion with him in the past?'

'No, absolutely not. I had been in his shop several times in the past and always found him to be very pleasant. I obviously must have caught him on a bad day.'

This was met with audible sighs coming from the Singh family contingent.

'Thank you, Mr Lamont,' says Russell Holstein. 'Now please just remain there as my learned friend may well have some questions for you.'

Miles is feeling quite pleased with his performance thus far, but then again, he has only experienced the warm-up act. The judge gives a nod to Joan Calvert as an indicator that the stage is now ready for her.

'Good afternoon, Mr Lamont. I would now like to go through your evidence in a little more detail than my learned friend. Initially, I would like to refer you once again to the night out you had a week or so prior to the assault on Harinder Singh. I believe you were in the Moves nightclub along with your friend, Johnny Morgan, is that correct?'

Miles somewhat timidly answers in the affirmative. His whole demeanour clearly shows that he does not relish questioning on this particular subject. Suddenly and without any prior warning, Joan Calvert goes for the jugular.

'So, you are a drug dealer?'

'No.'

'But you deal drugs – does that not make you a drug dealer?'

'Like most people of my age, I occasionally sample drugs, but I am not a dealer.'

'There is evidence from two different parties who have said that you are a dealer. So I suppose both of them are lying?'

'Yes, I suppose so,' he responds with a total lack of conviction and a touch of arrogance.

'And what motive would two independent people have for lying about your drug dealing, especially when one of them is your long-term friend?'

'I don't know.'

'Are you telling me that you do not sell drugs for money?'

'No, I do not,' says Miles, his feathers now being ruffled just a little.

'So, Gerry Smith, the employee of Moves nightclub who gave evidence that you sell drugs was not telling the truth, lying basically?'

'Yes, he was lying.'

'And why would he be lying?'

'I have no idea why he would make such allegations.'

'Your friend Johnny Morgan said you were dealing drugs in the club that night – I suppose he was lying, also?' Miles does not answer this question and the prosecution is happy to leave it out there. 'Why then would you be thrown out of the nightclub that particular evening?'

'I think I must have had a few too many drinks that evening as I don't really remember what happened.'

'Selective memory seems to be a common theme, it would appear, is it not?' Once again, Miles chooses not to respond. 'You have gone very quiet, Mr Lamont. Was it all a blur because you were drunk or under the influence of drugs, or both? Well, if you cannot recall what happened, then I assume we will just have to take the word of two key witnesses who both say that you assaulted the doorman at the nightclub, a certain Gerry Smith.'

'I suppose so,' answers Miles, very reluctantly. He is definitely starting to feel the heat.

'I understand that both Gerry Smith and the Moves nightclub, for reasons only known to themselves, chose not to have you reported to the police and subsequently charged. Had they chosen to pursue this matter, then your hitherto unblemished criminal record of which you seem so proud might well have been in jeopardy.' Joan Calvert hesitates for a few moments to allow the jury to fully digest what they have just heard before continuing. 'Now let me ask you to cast your mind back to the evening Harinder Singh was assaulted. You say that you arranged to pick up Johnny Morgan. You said when questioned by my learned friend that you had "a beer or two" before going out. I assume you were talking euphemistically?'

'I don't understand,' replies Miles.

'Let me re-phrase my question. I assume you were understating your actual beer consumption when you said you only had one or two beers.'

'No, I was telling the truth.'

'Well then, had you perhaps also taken some drugs?'

'No.'

'Is it not interesting that your friend was clearly aware that you were under the influence of drink or drugs, or both, and for that reason wanted out of the car? So was he lying?'

'I can only think he was mistaken.'

'And we have heard from another independent witness corroborating evidence from Johnny Morgan that your car actually mounted a pavement. Are we to assume that he, too, was lying or mistaken?'

'Maybe I was driving too fast and perhaps I did hit a kerb.'

'Yet another understatement. Come, come Mr Lamont. Let me remind you that you are under oath.' Joan Calvert walks towards the accused and stares at him for a minute or two, during which time he is almost visibly squirming. 'So, for the avoidance of doubt, Mr Lamont, it is your evidence now that all three of these witnesses are either lying or are mistaken.'

'Yes.'

'But you do accept that you were drinking beer while you were driving the car?

'Yes.'

'I have absolutely no doubt that the jury will attach whatever weight to your answers as they deem appropriate.'

'Objection, My Lord – not a question.'

'Objection sustained.'

'So you decided to stop off at Harry's corner shop for more beer. And is it not the case that when you arrived there that your friend Johnny Morgan took the beer can out of your hand and threw it out the window because he feared for his own safety?'

Miles looks towards his counsel before answering in the affirmative.

'And yet you had only consumed a couple of beers. One can only assume that you have an extremely low tolerance for alcohol. It is your evidence that when you did not get your way, you started to remonstrate with Mr Singh. What exactly did you say?'

'I cannot remember.'

'May I say once again that you appear to have a very selective memory.'

'Objection.'

'Sustained,' says Judge Drummond. 'Mrs Calvert, kindly restrict yourself to asking questions of the witness.'

'Yes, My Lord,' Joan Calvert replies before turning to Miles. 'Whatever you said must have made him really angry? Please tell us once again how he reacted.'

'He started throwing punches at me. I was frightened, and in order to defend myself, I also punched out and he fell to the ground.'

At this point, Aasha Singh can be heard sobbing in the public gallery.

'And this confrontation happened when Mr Singh was standing in the doorway, is that correct?'

'Yes.'

'Which begs the question, why did you not simply run off if you were genuinely frightened? You are nineteen years of age and Mr Harinder Singh was a man in his mid-sixties – would it not be safe to assume that you would be able to outrun him?'

Miles mumbles, 'Yes.'

'Could you please repeat that answer in a loud voice for the benefit of all the jurors?'

'Yes,' repeats Miles.

'Also, it is not as if you were cornered?'

'No,' says the defendant, rather quietly.

'Louder for the benefit of the jurors, please.'

'No,' repeats Miles Lamont, somewhat belligerently.

'So, what you are telling the court is that you could easily have run away but chose instead to seriously assault a much older man and then leave him bleeding in the doorway?'

Miles does not respond but looks soulfully towards Russell Holstein, secretly wishing he had taken his advice.

'May I ask your height and weight?'

'I am 1.83 metres and 80.1 kilos.'

'May it surprise you to know that Harinder Singh was 1.63 metres in height and only weighed 63 kilos?' Miles does not respond. Joan Calvert then repeats the measurements for maximum effect. 'Mr Lamont, are you honestly expecting this court to believe that a slightly built, smaller, older man about to go home to enjoy a family dinner actually beat you up?'

'That's what happened.' Responded Miles.

'Please tell the court what injuries you sustained?'

'I was punched in the face but mainly in the stomach which was badly bruised.'

'And did you show this bruising to the police?'

'No.'

'Did you show it to anyone?'

'No.'

'Did you take a photograph of the bruising that you could show to the court in support of your case?'

'No.'

'Just a few days later after the assault, you were interviewed by the police. You could have shown the bruising to them, could you not?

'I never thought of it.'

'You never thought of it, but you had the foresight to phone the emergency services from a phone that could not be traced and you had the foresight to hide your bloodstained shirt. Are you honestly expecting that anyone in this court would believe that you ever had bruising on your body?' (Joan Calvert is not expecting a response to this last question.) 'And you say that you were punched in the face. Was your nose bleeding?'

'No,' says Miles, becoming visibly more agitated the longer the cross-examination goes on.

'Was your lip bleeding?'

'No.'

'A little louder for the benefit of the jury.'

'I said, "no",' repeats Miles, now becoming extremely agitated.

'If it pleases My Lord, I would like to show the witness Exhibit Three, the shirt of the accused.' More sobbing comes from the public benches. 'Would you agree with me that this shirt has been saturated with blood?'

'Yes.'

'A little louder.'

'Yes,' Miles shouts out angrily, becoming increasingly rattled.

'Significantly, the forensics team examined this shirt and would you believe that all blood samples are those of the late Harinder Singh?' Miles opts not to respond. 'Are you honestly expecting the court to believe that you were beaten up and yet there is not one drop of your blood on your own shirt? Talking of your shirt, we have heard police evidence to the effect that you had hidden your shirt under other clothes in a corner of your wardrobe. Is that correct?'

'No, I had just thrown it in.'

'So, if the police say that your shirt was hidden in a corner under other clothes, then they are lying also? Come, come, Mr Lamont. Please remember that you are under oath. Your bloodstained shirt was hidden under clean clothes in a corner of your wardrobe. Surely you would normally put soiled clothes in a laundry basket? I believe you deliberately hid the bloodstained shirt out of view, is that not so?'

'You can believe what you bloody well like, I don't care,' shouts Miles angrily, unravelling by the minute and hardly endearing himself to the jury.

'Was this the temper that you displayed when you assaulted Harinder Singh?'

'Oh, you are such a smart ass, aren't you?' barks Miles. At this, Walter Bryson and Russell Holstein exchange a knowing glance and Judge Drummond intervenes by telling the accused to show respect to Mrs Calvert. The look of utter disdain on the face of Miles Lamont is clear for all to see.

'So basically, virtually everyone who has given evidence against you, including your friend, has been lying to incriminate you. Are you honestly expecting the jurors to believe that?'

Miles chooses not to respond, but Joan Calvert knows that she has him on the ropes and is eager to land a final telling blow.

'Mr Lamont, I put it to you that on the sixth of August 2021 you were under the influence of alcohol and or drugs and you did viciously assault Harinder Singh in a completely unprovoked attack and did kick him in the head, ultimately causing his death. Is that not the true course of events?'

Once again there is no response from the accused.

'My Lord, I rest my case for the Crown.'

'Mr Holstein, do you wish to re-examine this witness?' asks the Judge.

'No, My Lord.' Russell Holstein is very conscious that his client is pretty much a loose cannon and does not want to take the risk of him imploding any more than he already has.

'Very well, ladies and gentlemen,' says Judge Drummond, 'I think this would be a convenient time to bring matters to a close for the day. We will reconvene proceedings tomorrow morning at ten o'clock when you will hear the final addresses from both the Crown and the defence.'

Chapter 81

First to put their case to the jurors is the prosecution, represented by Joan Calvert.

'Good morning, ladies and gentlemen. I thank you for your patience and endurance during this trial. You will be pleased to hear that I will try to be relatively brief because from where I am standing, the facts of this case are fairly clear.

'On the one hand, we have a man in his sixties, a pillar of society, a family man, clearly loved and respected within his community – a man who has never had a brush with the law. This man was closing up his family business for the evening to go home to join his wife for dinner, she having left the shop just a short time earlier. Very soon thereafter, he was discovered lying in his shop doorway in a pool of his own blood, his phone ringing in his pocket. The missed calls were from his wife enquiring as to why he was late for his evening meal.

'On the other hand, we have the accused. A plucky nineteen-year-old driving about in his flashy car with a private registration plate whilst at the same time also drinking beer. We have heard strong, credible, independent evidence of his car having mounted the pavement, exhibiting a total disregard for human life.

'Also make no mistake about it, ladies and gentlemen, Miles

Lamont is a man with violent tendencies. We heard evidence to this effect from Gerry Smith, the doorman at Moves nightclub as corroborated by Johnny Morgan. Also, as recently as yesterday, you experienced evidence of his short temper while under cross-examination. Add to this his alcohol and probable drug intake and we have a quite deadly cocktail – literally.'

'And what of compassion – has he exhibited any? I think not. Having given his victim a very severe beating, his thoughts were only for himself as he immediately fled the scene, leaving his victim in a pool of blood.'

'Had the true course of events been as suggested by him, would he actually have rushed away from the scene so quickly or would he not have been more likely to have immediately tried to secure medical assistance for the victim? Ladies and gentlemen, that is for you to decide. And when he did eventually phone the emergency services, he was sufficiently devious as not to even leave his name. Does that not tell its own story? If he had been assaulted to the extent that he feared for his safety, would there not have been his own bloodstains on his shirt? Yes, that very shirt that he tried to hide – unsuccessfully – in his wardrobe.'

'You have heard in evidence of the disparity in the height and weight of the accused and the deceased. If you still have any doubts about who was the aggressor and who was the victim, surely this factor alone will allay those doubts.'

'In addition, it has been made abundantly clear that the defendant, had he actually been under threat, could easily have retreated. We have heard evidence to the effect that it was actually the victim who was "boxed in" at the shop doorway.'

'Ladies and gentlemen of the jury, I have taken up sufficient of your time. I would hope that, like me, you consider the evidence against the accused to be nothing short of overwhelming. Consequently, I would invite you to return a unanimous verdict of "guilty" to the charge of murder.'

Russell Holstein is next to put his case to the jurors. His arguments are pretty much in line with his address at the first trial, however seemingly with a little less gusto. It is almost as if Russell Holstein is aggrieved with his client for insisting on taking the stand, completely ignoring very specific advice to the contrary. Perhaps even more significantly, Holstein wants a not guilty verdict for reasons of personal pride and to further enhance his reputation, and his client's stubbornness is alienating against this. Whatever motivational factors are at play, the address on behalf of the defendant is very short and sweet:

'Ladies and gentlemen of the jury, you have now heard all the evidence and very shortly you will be asked to consider it in its entirety before arriving at a verdict. The reality of this case is that none of us actually knows what happened that fateful evening. We have two separate accounts, both very differing. You heard from the accused yesterday. Let it be known that he did not require to give evidence, he did so entirely of his own free will as he was keen to let you hear his side of the story. Yes, he was becoming a little irate and hot under the collar when being questioned by my learned friend. Wouldn't you if you were being accused of a crime of this enormity and one of which you are not guilty? You also have to take account of the age of the defendant; he is still a teenager and should perhaps be forgiven for being somewhat impetuous in these very serious circumstances. Yes, ladies and gentlemen, it is just possible you might think that Miles Lamont is guilty of murder. But might is simply not good enough. This court requires a higher standard of proof. If you have a reasonable doubt that my client is innocent, then you are obliged to return a verdict of "not guilty" and I would invite you so to do. Please do not consider convicting based only on circumstantial evidence. Thank you for your time and patience.'

Judge Hector Drummond then gives a standard charge to the jury before dismissing them to start their deliberations. Initially, he warns the jurors to ignore anything they might have read online or in newspapers or on television. Once again, the accent is upon the jurors being the masters of the facts whereas Judge Drummond is the arbiter of the law. Also, further emphasis is placed on the jury requiring to be satisfied beyond reasonable doubt if they are going to convict. He emphasises that this is not a fanciful or whimsical doubt, but rather a doubt that any reasonable man in reasonable circumstances would deem to be valid. With these last instructions still ringing in their ears, the jury duly retire.

Chapter 82

Alan and Christine Wright – aka the Winters couple – have settled well into life in the Costa del Sol. They are fortunate that they have enough illegitimate cash tucked away that they do not have to work for the foreseeable future. Also, they are paying their rent by cash and are generally trying to keep as low a profile as possible. Alan still has a shaved head but has now grown a fairly lengthy beard, the combination making him almost completely unrecognisable from his former self. Equally, Christine bears little resemblance to Carol Winters with her now short blonde hair and glasses with clear lenses.

They are currently enjoying a relatively quiet life. While Christine is working hard at perfecting her tan, Alan is trying to improve his golf handicap. Although life appears fairly stress-free, they do find it a little aimless, and in time they are thinking they would like to return to work of some description. They simply miss the adrenalin flow. However, remaining under the radar is always going to be uppermost in their minds. Having said that, they feel that the chances of them being recognised or apprehended are very remote as they have been extremely careful to cover their tracks and have left absolutely nothing to chance. It is as if Andy and Carol Winters have never existed.

Just when all appears to be going smoothly in their new life in the sun, a minor tragedy strikes. Christine had inadvertently left the front door of their apartment open and the love of their lives, little Oli the miniature dachshund, has managed to escape. They are totally distraught. He could only have been away for a maximum of forty-five minutes before they realised he had gone, but in that time, he could have travelled quite some distance – even with those tiny legs. They choose to leave the house and both run in opposite directions, shouting his name and also asking their neighbours if they have seen him. Eventually about an hour later, they meet up back at the house having both been unsuccessful. Further searches that evening also prove fruitless. They are totally devastated. Also, it is so utterly frustrating for them as they are reluctant to go to the police for very obvious reasons.

Chapter 83

The jury take their place in the jury room. The appointment of their foreperson is a fairly straightforward affair. Paula Watson, a personnel manager working within a large household-named retail company in the city centre promptly proposes herself for the role. So confidently does she speak that others who may have intended putting themselves forward for the position choose to slip quietly into the background. Paula is elected unopposed.

'Let's get started then, shall we?' says Paula in a very business-like, no-nonsense manner. 'I suggest we test the temperature of the room by going round the table asking each of you in turn how you wish to vote, or indeed whether you are still undecided.' Paula starts the voting by stating 'guilty' and then she goes around the table in a clockwise direction. Ultimately the votes are as follows:

Guilty – 9
Not guilty – 0
Undecided – 3

Significantly or otherwise, the three who are undecided are among the youngest on the jury. Paula continues with her no-nonsense approach by stating the case, as she sees it, in favour of a guilty verdict. She is very persuasive and utterly convincing, and within about half an hour, the three abstainers have collapsed like a pack of cards. They have reached a unanimous verdict in almost record time. One could be forgiven for thinking that Paula Watson has an engagement this evening that she is determined to keep. Before one can say, 'guilty as sin', she notifies the clerk of court that they have arrived at their decision and it is unanimous.

Word quickly spreads around the court building that the jurors have arrived at a decision. Coffees are gulped down and toilets are hastily visited. The press and those with a vested interest all speculate as to the significance of the jury having arrived at a verdict so quickly. In their various groups, they all pile into the courtroom trying to secure a good viewing position. There is a buzz of conversation and anticipation and the clerk of court has to demand order in the court. Accessing the court from the hidden steps that emerge out of the bowels of the Old Bailey, the defendant enters the dock and all eyes are set upon him.

Three heavy raps signal the arrival of the judge. Once he is in situ, the jurors are asked if they have appointed a foreperson.

'We have,' says Paula Watson. 'I have been appointed foreperson.'

'And have you reached a verdict on which you are all agreed?'

'We have, My Lord.'

The defendant is asked to stand up.

'Do you find the defendant guilty or not guilty of the murder of Harinder Singh?'

'We find the defendant, guilty.'

Immediately there is a cacophony of cheers, jeers and a general rabble. Judge Drummond tries to bring some order to proceedings. Derek Lamont is instantly removed from the court for shouting profanities. Olivia Lamont is slumped in her seat and is sobbing uncontrollably while being comforted by Mel. Meeta and Aasha Singh are also extremely emotional, albeit for quite different reasons. Chas strikes the air with his fist in triumph. DI Ronald shakes hands with both DC Green and DC Gordon in recognition of a job well done. There is a knowing look between Walter Bryson and Russell Holstein which says, 'what are we supposed to do if our client chooses to disregard our advice.' Bryson's mind is racing as he vividly recalls Derek Lamont's threat to him in the event of a guilty verdict being returned. His whole career is endangered, not to mention his freedom.

In the meantime, Miles Lamont cannot believe what has just happened. He is weak at the knees and feels physically sick. He looks around to the public gallery and he is drawn to the image of Chas Singh. This time around, Chas is the one who is doing the leering - and big time.

Once the court has been brought to order, Judge Drummond addresses the defendant.

'Miles Lamont, you have been found guilty of the ultimate crime of murder. You have taken another man's life in a heartless, cold-blooded and brutal manner and have left his loving family in a state of total devastation. You have also brought shame on your own family. You have devastated those close to you who will have thought you incapable of such shocking, mindful violence. Sentencing will be deferred for two weeks. Take him down.'

Finally, Judge Drummond thanks the jury. 'Ladies and gentlemen of the jury, the trial is now at an end and it only remains for me to now formally discharge you from your duties and obligations. May I thank you for your kind attention throughout this trial? You have played a most vital role in proceedings. You are now formally discharged and are free to go.'

Chapter 84

Lara Watkins, a typical happy-go-lucky seven-year-old girl, is playing in her back garden with her dolls. She and her parents moved to Spain from the UK three years ago, opting for a complete life change. Fortunately her mum and dad, Peter and Fiona, both had jobs whereby they were able to work remotely. The weather was one very influential factor and a much slower pace of life also held appeal. Furthermore, they relished the idea that their daughter would grow up bilingual which would do her no harm in her future life. When moving to Spain, they looked at various areas before settling on the Costa del Sol, more particularly Estepona where they purchased a modern townhouse. They had been charmed by the buzz of Estepona's quaint and enchanting old town and also the choice of sandy beaches.

Suddenly, Lara has the most unexpected but welcome of visitors. She excitedly calls to her parents in the house.

'Mum, Dad, look – a sausage dog!'

Her parents come out to find their daughter lying on the ground being licked to death by a happy looking, tail-wagging miniature dachshund.

'Look, Mum, he really likes me. Please, please, please may I keep him? Please say I can.'

Upon checking, he has a blue collar and a bone-shaped, silver, metal name tag bearing the name 'Oli.'

'I am really sorry, but you can't as he will belong to someone else and they will be upset to have lost him. We will have to take Oli to the local police station to allow them to trace his owners.'

'But Mum, look, he loves me and I love him.'

'No means no,' voices Fiona Watkins.

At this point, Lara puts on one of her repertoire of facial expressions, one her parents are more than familiar with, namely the 'huff look'.

Peter Watkins, whom Lara can usually wrap around her little finger, says, 'We will have to take the dog to the police station. If he is not claimed within a certain period of time, then perhaps we might be allowed to keep him, but that is very unlikely given that he has a name tag.' Fiona then gives her husband one of her 'you're such a softy' looks.

That afternoon, they jump in their car, her mum and dad in the front seat while Lara sits in the back stroking the ultra-cute sausage dog on her lap. Within the hour, Oli is left in the police station and a tearful Lara and her parents are on their way home. The police are quite confident the owners will be traced. As well as the name tag, the fact that it is a miniature and of the long-haired variety gives the dog a certain uniqueness.

Chapter 85

It is standard practice for the counsel and instructing solicitor to visit the defendant in the cells, following a guilty verdict. As one can imagine, it is sometimes not the most pleasant of tasks, but nevertheless, Walter Bryson and Russell Holstein make the necessary arrangements. They are shown to a dedicated cell for this purpose, and a short time later, their client is led in. He has obviously been crying and is visibly upset. However, his mood rapidly changes to one of anger. He is wanting to kick out at somebody, looking for anyone to blame and why not his defence team? He does not hold back.

'After I was questioned by that bitch, why did you not re-examine me to let me answer all those false allegations that were made against me?'

'I am more than happy to answer that. In fact, I will answer your question very specifically,' responds Russell Holstein. 'We could not have advised you any more clearly not to take the stand. I told you, Mr Bryson told you and your father also tried unsuccessfully to persuade you to refrain from giving evidence. But no, you knew better than us. We had a winnable case and you absolutely blew it and completely alienated the jury against you. So the last thing I was going to do was give you the opportunity to tie the noose any tighter. That is why I did not re-examine you.'

'I want you to appeal this case on my behalf,' says Miles.

On this occasion, it is again Russell Holstein who takes up the baton. 'It is entirely up to you whether you choose to appeal your conviction or not, but if you do, I will not be acting on your behalf. I am not prepared to act for clients who totally ignore very clear advice issued both by myself and your solicitor. I have obviously not had time yet to advise your dad of this decision, but I will do so at the very first opportunity. I will appear for your sentencing, and then that is me finished with your case.'

Walter Bryson keeps a diplomatic silence, neither associating nor disassociating with Holstein's remarks, being ever conscious of the earlier threat made by Derek Lamont.

Miles is becoming more and more angry with every passing moment and looking as if he is about to combust. He is wanting to blame anyone but himself for the fact that he is going to have to spend a sizeable part of his future life behind bars.

'To hell with you both, then. For my appeal, I will employ a defence team who will actually look after my interests.'

At this point, both Walter Bryson and Russell Holstein leave the cell with oaths ringing in their ears.

Chapter 86

Not surprisingly, the Wrights have had a sleepless night worrying about their beloved pooch. It is the morning after Oli went missing and the Wrights' doorbell rings – for the very first time. They both freeze on the spot. Who could this possibly be? Nobody knows where they live. It is what they have always dreaded. In absolute trepidation, Christine answers the door. Upon seeing a policewoman in uniform, she feels weak at the knees. It transpires the policewoman is actually an immediate neighbour. Her English is exceptionally good, although heavily accented.

'Hello, my name is Maria. I live in the apartment below. By any chance, have you lost your little dog?'

'Yes,' says a massively relieved Christine.

'And Oli is its name?'

'Yes.'

'Someone has handed him into the Estepona Police Station, and when I arrived at work yesterday afternoon, I thought I recognised him. I am just going on duty now, so please call by anytime this morning with his pet passport and I will have him there for you. He should already have been taken to the dog pound, but we loved him so much we kept him in the police station overnight.' They thank her and say goodbye. Their relief is almost palpable.

Alan and Christine Wright have very mixed feelings – absolute delight that Oli has been found but real apprehension about entering a police station, for very obvious reasons. Is it possible that they could be walking into a trap – or are their imaginations just running wild? Thank goodness that they had the foresight to order a Spanish dog passport from Harry Gibbs. After some discussion, they decide, lest they might be recognised as a 'wanted couple', that it would be best if only one of them goes to the police to claim him. Given that Christine is the more nervous of the two, they determine that Alan should be the one to go, but even he is extremely apprehensive. As it happens, it turns out to be pretty much a formality and all their worries and concerns are proved to be unfounded. When Alan enters the police station in trepidation, the first person he meets is a uniformed officer called Enrique. He is grey-haired with strands of white and is of an age where he would soon be approaching retirement. He has a benign expression and a warm manner. Fortunately he, too, can speak a little English. Within a minute or two, Maria appears with the bold Oli, his tail wagging so much it is at risk of becoming detached from his body. All Alan has to do is show Oli's passport to her – deal done. Another obstacle has been overcome and there is an overwhelming sense of relief all around.

Chapter 87

Although the trial has finished and a satisfactory conclusion arrived at, there are still a number of loose ends to be tied up as far as DI Ronald is concerned. One such loose end, and a very major one, relates to the question of jury tampering. At the start of the trial proper, Paul Webster's daughter was targeted. The point is that the Winters couple must have had prior knowledge of who was on the jury list for that day, suggesting an inside job. With this in mind, DI Ronald again contacts William Barnes the Director of Prosecutions in order to secure a shortlist of the names of those within the service who have this knowledge at their disposal. This information is very readily made available and there are three potentials on the list. DI Ronald promptly makes arrangements to interview all three as voluntary attenders. Rather than go to their office, she prefers to interview them in the police station to take them out of their own comfort zone.

Interviewee number one is a woman in her early sixties with one eye on retirement. She has been a loyal and reliable member of the prosecution service for some twenty-five years. She is extremely forthcoming and forthright when questioned. DI Ronald is one hundred percent satisfied in her own mind that she is free from suspicion.

Interviewee number two is a young married man in his late twenties with a young daughter of eighteen months. It is so obvious that his family is his whole world. While he might be finding finances somewhat tight having now to survive on one income, in the valued opinion of DI Ronald, he is not the type of man to be foolish enough to jeopardise his precious family life.

Call it intuition, but as soon as interviewee number three enters the room, DI Ronald says to herself, 'Now we are in business.' She can immediately see the apprehension in his face, and his body language is far from convincing. It is perfectly obvious that he does not want to be there. He is far from being comfortable in his own skin.

'Have you any idea why you are here today?' says DI Ronald.

'No, my boss just asked me to attend because you wanted to ask me about some trial or other.'

'Some trial or other?' asks DI Ronald. 'So you have no idea which trial it is? Go on, have a guess.'

'No idea,' he repeats.

'Let me help you then. I am here to question you regarding the Miles Lamont case. Does that mean anything to you?'

'Yes, I remember the name,' he says whilst becoming redder in the face.

'You don't seem very comfortable answering my questions.'

No response.

'I said, you don't seem very comfortable answering my questions.'

'I am just not used to it.'

'Ok,' says DI Ronald, bluffing. 'We know that you handed out jury information in the Lamont case which subsequently resulted in witness tampering. Also, we will be able to prove it. So you have two choices: You can continue to refuse to cooperate, and when you are ultimately convicted – and you will be – then you will be going to prison for a very long time. Alternatively, you can come clean and I will let it be known to the Crown Office that you assisted us in our inquiries and your sentence will be much lighter. It is your choice entirely.'

DI Ronald knows that he is on the point of capitulation and so she remains quiet, thereby allowing the reality of his situation to completely sink in.

'Ok, I will co-operate, but I want you to assure me that you will put in a word for me.'

'I promise.'

Before long, he confesses to having sold a juror list and is arrested and cautioned. He is a little reluctant to reveal his contact, but eventually after some more gentle persuasion, the name 'Kenny Freeman' is given up – the private investigator who is known to the local police. The net is definitely closing in.

By the way, interviewee number three is a certain Michael Harding.

Chapter 88

It is early morning, about 8.00 am, when there is yet another unexpected knock at the Winters' door in Estepona. But on this occasion, it does not relate to Oli. As before, the door is opened with trepidation, but this time around it is not unfounded. One of the officers is Enrique whom they met on the last occasion, but his demeanour is quite different – much more sombre.

'Mr and Mrs Winters, we would like you to accompany us to the police station,' says Enrique in a very matter-of-fact and unemotional tone. The second they are referred to as 'Mr and Mrs Winters', they are obviously aware that their cover has been broken. Their race has been run. They totally succumb and are taken down to the local police station along with Oli, who this time around is pound-bound.

They felt so sure that they had completely covered their tracks, especially since they look nothing like their former selves. When they arrive at the police station, they again come across Maria. As she speaks pretty good English, Andy Winters asks how on earth the police managed to identify them. They seem genuinely surprised by the answer they receive.

'When Oli was first handed in to the police station, he was automatically taken to the local vet to see if he had been chipped. It transpired that he had and is registered with the National Pet Chip Registry which revealed your original names and your UK address. This raised some suspicion and then it came to light after checking with Interpol that you are both wanted by the police in the UK.'.

Andy and Carol Winters are so immersed in the thought that they are going to be incarcerated for a lengthy period of time that they have not thought of their beloved Oli. They have nobody back home who could look after him. The irony is not lost on them that had it not been for Oli they would still be free as birds. Being an animal lover herself, Maria has some sympathy for them, despite their alleged past indiscretions.

'I know a loving family who would most probably look after him, and it would make one little seven-year-old girl very, very happy.' Carol Winters just about manages a smile through the floods of tears.

DI Ronald is absolutely delighted to receive a call to the effect that Andy and Carol Winters have been apprehended. In no time at all, she applies for an extradition order and makes plans to fly to Spain to arrest them and then escort them back to the UK.

Chapter 89

DI Ronald had instructed DCs Green and Gordon to apprehend the private detective, Kenny Freeman. Unannounced, they visit his downtown, one-room, hole-in-the-wall office. He is sitting at his desk drinking from a half bottle of whisky and is surrounded by some randomly placed files, an over-filled ashtray and the remains of his lunch. If searching for something positive to say, at least his office surroundings are in keeping with his personal appearance. He is then taken down to the police station to be interviewed by DI Ronald and chooses not to have legal representation.

'Is your name Kenny Freeman?' asks DI Ronald.

'No comment.'

'What is the nature of your business?'

'No comment.'

'Do you know a Michael Harding?'

'No comment.'

'What is your relationship with Michael Harding?'

'No comment.'

'We have already interviewed Michael Harding and he has come clean about everything, so there is no point in remaining silent.'

'No comment.'

'Do you know a Derek Lamont?'

'No comment.'

Eventually, DI Ronald decides she has had enough. She does not consider she has sufficient evidence to charge him at this stage, and in any event, she has bigger fish to fry. With this in mind, she terminates the interview but decides to let him stew in the interview room for a short while before releasing him. However, she is conscious that she somehow has to find a link between Kenny Freeman and Derek Lamont.

Chapter 90

Armed with a European Arrest Warrant, DI Ronald takes a flight to Malaga and arrests and charges Andy and Carol Winters – otherwise known as Alan and Christine Wright – and duly returns with them to the UK. Inwardly, she reluctantly has to admire their art of disguise. She would never have been able to recognise them from their original photographs. Andy Winters is placed on remand in HMP Belmarsh while Carol Winters is accommodated in HMP Bronzefield. This is convenient for DI Ronald as they can now be interviewed on a 'divide and separate' basis. The evidence against them in relation to the abduction of young Emma Webster is fairly overwhelming, especially in relation to Carol Winters. The statement from Emma and the video evidence are both pretty damning. However, it is nothing more than supposition that Andy Winters is in fact Balaclava Man.

Both interviews are being conducted by DI Ronald and DC Gordon. After the caution and the usual preliminaries, the interviewers get down to business. Firstly they interview Andy Winters.

'Is your full name Andrew Winters, known as Andy Winters?' asks DI Ronald.

'No comment.'

'Did you previously reside at fourteen Walker Avenue, Westwood, London.'

'No comment.'

'Do you know Paul and Rita Webster?'

'No comment.'

'Do you know a child called Emma Webster?'

'No comment.'

'Did you and your wife abduct said Emma Webster?'

'No comment.'

'Did you restrain said Emma Webster against her will at your house at fourteen Walker Avenue?'

'No comment.'

'Did you and your wife recently change your names to Alan and Christine Wright?'

'No comment.'

'On or about the sixth of January 2022, did you and your wife leave the UK in order to avoid arrest and set up home in Estepona in the Costa del Sol, southern Spain?'

'No comment.'

'Let's go back a little further in time, shall we? Where were you on the twelfth of November 2021, the date of the attack on a certain Johnny Morgan?'

'No comment.'

'Do you know a Johnny Morgan?'

'No comment.'

'I put it to you that on the twelfth of November 2021, you did attack Johnny Morgan with a knife in Mortimer Lane in London.'

'No comment.'

At this point, DI Ronald formally terminates the interview and, without showing any emotion, she and DC Gordon leave the interview room in silence.

Later that afternoon, they interview Mrs Winters at HMP Bronzefield. She has agreed with her husband that they both will say absolutely nothing. She is working herself into a frenzy as she waits to be interviewed. The thought of her perhaps having a long stretch in prison truly terrifies her.

Eventually she is advised that DI Ronald and DC Gordon have

arrived to interview her. They both enter the interview room in a very confident and upbeat manner – intentionally on their part.

What on earth has Andy said to them? She wonders to herself.

DI Ronald switches on the recording tape and attends to all the formalities before getting down to the serious business.

'Well, Mrs Winters, or should I say "Sarah" or perhaps even "Christine?" Well, what an interesting chat we have just had with your husband. I am pleased and relieved that we now know all there is to know and this interview is virtually redundant. Feel free to stop me or correct me if I get anything wrong or miss out anything.'

Carol Winters feels completely crestfallen.

'Okay, Kenny Freeman, the private detective, managed to illegally procure a witness list for the trial of Miles Lamont. This he obtained from a corrupt court officer by the name of Michael Harding. On the morning of the first day of the trial, your husband Andy was at court – we even have him on CCTV! Once he discovered who had been selected for jury duty, you were able to select your target, namely Emma Webster.'

'The following morning, Andy slashed one of Rita Webster's tyres, thereby making her late for school. Once Andy tipped you off, you had the all-clear to go to the school to collect Emma under your Sarah persona. And of course, by mentioning to the school staff that Rita had a puncture, your credibility was enhanced. In the meantime, Andy put one of a number of terrifying notes through the Websters' letterbox, threatening to murder little Emma if they did not comply with your wishes. Of course, copies of all these threatening letters are now in our possession. Returning to your home at fourteen Walker Avenue, Westwood, London, you kept poor little Emma in a bedroom with the window boarded up, only allowing her out to go to the toilet. She still has Eddie the Teddy, a sad reminder of her period of enforced solitude.'

By this time, Carol Winters has broken down into tears. Not surprisingly, DI Ronald does not show one iota of sympathy. It is perfectly clear that her visible signs of distress are for her own plight, nothing to do with what little Emma had to endure.

'Once you had received word that the desired verdict had been achieved, you then set about returning Emma to her parents. We have video of you in the vicinity of the playground. Also, young Emma has identified you – you were wearing a pair of blue jeans and a pink tee shirt. She has also identified the room in your house where she was detained, the one with the boarded-up window. Not only that, she occasionally heard you talking with Andy on the telephone.'

'Do I really need to go any further? Your race is run. As you can tell, we have all the information we require. You now have two very clear options. Firstly, you can sit here in silence and then ultimately be convicted. Or alternatively, you can confirm everything to us that we already know. If you choose the latter, then it will not only save us a lot of time, but the judge will take it into account when sentencing. I know for sure what I would do if I were in your shoes.'

Totally convinced, erroneously, that her husband has revealed all, Carol Winters does exactly that. She has gone for the bait, hook, line and sinker.

There are still a couple of loose ends as far as DI Ronald is concerned. While Carol Winters has made a full confession, there are two significant omissions. Firstly, she refused to disclose who she and her husband were working for. And secondly, no progress has been made in relation to the identity of 'balaclava man'.

While Carol Winters has been tricked into a confession, DI Ronald has been very careful with her wording and has not actually stated that her husband had already confessed. Carol Winters has simply assumed this to be the case, in light of the knowledge that DI Ronald has imparted.

Chapter 91

Two weeks after the retrial

The day has eventually arrived, the day that Miles Lamont will be sentenced. The court is packed with all the usual suspects, among these is the Singh family who have closed their shop for the day, the Lamonts, Felicity and Constance, and DI Jean Ronald. Interestingly, two or three of the original jury members are also in attendance. And of course there are those playing a part in proceedings, namely Hector Drummond the judge, Joan Calvert on behalf of the prosecution and, of course, the defence team of Walter Bryson and Russell Holstein. Once the formalities have been attended to, it is for Joan Calvert to take the lead.

'My Lord, the facts of this case are extremely straightforward. The accused, Miles Lamont, has been found guilty of the murder of Harinder Singh outside his place of work on the sixth of August 2021. The evidence has shown that he viciously attacked the now deceased by punching him and then kicking him on the head with such ferocity that it caused the death of the said Harinder Singh. Evidence has shown that the defendant was under the influence of drink and drugs on the evening in question. This is of course no excuse for his actions.

There was also earlier evidence of the defendant showing a propensity to violence, establishing that this was not an isolated incident. This case is all the more disturbing given that the victim was a law-abiding citizen going about his daily business and one who has left behind a family devastated in grief. It is also significant that after having carried out the cowardly and heinous crime, the accused rushed off with apparently no concern whatsoever for the welfare of his victim. My Lord, I would invite you to take all these circumstances into account when sentencing the defendant.'

'Thank you, Mrs Calvert.' Judge Drummond then looks to Russell Holstein on behalf of the defendant.

'I thank you, My Lord. As my learned friend has stated, this has been an extremely straightforward case. I think we have to remind ourselves that Miles Lamont at nineteen years of age is still only a youth and still has a lot of maturing to do. How many of us did stupid things when we were teenagers, albeit admittedly nothing on this kind of level? One momentary loss of control and loss of temper and he is now facing very serious consequences.

My Lord, let me accentuate a fact which arose during the trial. Unlike so many who appear before My Lord, Miles Lamont is appearing in court for the very first time – he is a first offender. Also, to his credit, since leaving school, he has remained in gainful employment. Yes, it was quite correct to say that being under the influence of drink does not in any way serve as an excuse, but I think it fair to say that had it not been for its consumption, Miles Lamont would not be standing before this court here today and Harinder Singh would still be alive. My client now freely accepts that he has an addictive personality and he has undertaken to have treatment (if available to him) during his period of incarceration.

'Finally, my client has asked me to formally express apologies on his behalf to the Singh family for the pain and heartache he has brought upon them.'

'Thank you, Mr Holstein. Would the defendant please stand. Mr Lamont, you have been found guilty by a jury of your peers of murder. I have listened very carefully to what my learned friends have just said. I do accept that you are young and also that you come before this court as a first offender. However, notwithstanding, you have been found guilty of the most vicious, unprovoked, cowardly and heinous attack on an older man and you must be punished accordingly. Consequently, I sentence you to custody for life with a minimum term order of fifteen years before an application can be made for release on parole. Take him down.'

The announcement of the sentence causes chaos in the court. Miles Lamont instantly collapses, his legs suddenly giving way. Olivia Lamont shrieks in anguish while her husband shouts a vile oath at the judge and is once again removed from the court. Chas Singh is cheering enthusiastically while both Joan Calvert and DI Jean Ronald allow themselves smiles of self-satisfaction. In the press box, the newspaper reporters are all scribbling furiously before exiting the court to join the photographers.

Epilogue

One year later

Hi, it is Chas here once again, one year after that fateful evening. I am pleased to say that The Singh Family is still a very close family. The pain of our loss still exists but gradually eases as the days and weeks go by. Our dad's name is still above the door of our corner shop and he will continue to be fondly remembered by family, friends and customers alike. Business has been going from strength to strength and I feel I have matured so much in my new role of decision-maker.

Celebrations have recently been taking place in the family as my sister, Aasha, has passed her degree exams and is now officially a doctor. Our mum, Meeta, felt extremely proud at the university graduation ceremony, although it was inevitably a bittersweet experience.

Yes, there were plenty of tears, some of joy, others of regret, due to the fact that the head of the family could not be there to co-celebrate.

#

And otherwise...

Miles Lamont is once again in HMP Belmarsh but this time not on remand. Within the first couple of months, he was subjected to ridicule by some other inmates as well as being the victim of a few minor beatings. However, things have been improving slightly as one or two 'newbies' have arrived in the prison and fortunately this has taken the spotlight away from him. Also, he has a cellmate who is also relatively new to the prison system, and so there is some benefit in being kindred spirits. He has at least fourteen years left in prison to contemplate what might have been. A punishment that is very well deserved.

Derek Lamont's business, both the legitimate side and the not so, still appear to be producing healthy profits. One might have anticipated that given the circumstances he would perhaps have withdrawn from the drugs element of the business, but not so. Derek Lamont has delusions of invincibility. However, matters have depreciated dramatically on the matrimonial side. An already fragile marriage could not withstand the ignominy of their son being jailed for murder. Olivia blames her husband for their son being incarcerated, and perhaps not without foundation, given that Derek conveniently turned a blind eye to his son's wayward ways. The bottom line is that Olivia has moved out of the matrimonial home and into a luxury apartment. She has also contacted a London hot-shot matrimonial lawyer to ensure that Derek will be divested of a very sizeable proportion of his wealth. Relations have become so vitriolic between them that Olivia has even threatened to highlight her husband's drug dealing if he fails to meet her not insubstantial financial demands.

Mel Lamont is now married to her boyfriend, Stuart. Her decision to get married and set up home was accelerated because she could not bear to live with her parents any longer due to the incessant feuding between them and the toxic atmosphere which existed. So Mel actually moved out of the house before her mum did. In normal circumstances, her parents would have wanted a lavish, posh and flamboyant wedding for their daughter. However, given Miles's incarceration and the fact that relationships were so bad between them, this luxury was foregone. It was a rather tame affair in a registry office with a very modest reception in a local hotel. Mel had hoped that her parents might have buried the hatchet for that one day, even just for her sake, but sadly that was not to be. So there was a bit of an atmosphere between them at the wedding, but Mel and Stuart were determined that they would not allow it to detract from their enjoyment of their big day. Meanwhile, 'Hair by Mel' continues to go from strength to strength and Mel now employs four stylists and a junior.

One thing you can credit Walter Bryson with is staying power. While people around him have been falling like skittles, he continues to successfully operate illegally without falling foul of the law enforcers. His extremely profitable business now allows him more time to enjoy relaxation on his newly acquired yacht moored in the South of France. There is just one little cloud hanging over his head. The threat made by Derek Lamont to expose him has never completely vanished, although with every day, week and month that passes, it seems less likely that he will act on it.

Constance and Felicity continue to be social butterflies and are spending even more time with Olivia since she is now a free spirit. The three of them are having regular girly nights out usually with glasses of bubbly in hand. This in turn is causing friction for Felicity in her marriage to David, who is questioning the fact that his wife seems to be living the life of a singleton.

Johnny Morgan has detached himself completely from the Lamont family. The murder and its subsequent fallout ironically had a beneficial effect on him as it served as an opportunity to reset his life. Not only did he knuckle down and concentrate on his studies in order to secure his degree, but also he met the love of his life. Yes, he and Linda are now very much an item and it would appear that she is a very good influence on him.

After such a long time, the Webster Family is still trying to recover from the trauma of Emma's abduction. One year on and all three of them are still receiving counselling. One repercussion of the abduction is that Paul and Rita hardly let Emma out of their sight and have become so, so protective. As Emma becomes a little older, this may bring its own problems, but in all the circumstances, their reaction is quite understandable if not inevitable. The Websters are in receipt of frequent reports from their daughter's school, and it appears that she is still showing post-trauma symptoms, but thankfully they are reducing in severity and regularity.

The career of DI Jean Ronald continues to spiral upwards and it is universally anticipated that she is destined for greater things. Very sadly her dad passed away. However, it was a blessing at the end of the day as his health had depreciated so rapidly that he did not recognise his daughter and occasionally not even his wife. He had absolutely no quality of life. Being an only child, Jean has been a tremendous support for her mum whilst still showing great commitment to her job. However, she is now able to spread her affections in three different directions, namely her mum, her work and her fiancé. Yes, her relationship with DC Andrew Gordon has gone from strength to strength and they intend being married in the summer.

DC Janet Green has continued to impress and it is anticipated that she will gradually move up the ranks. Initially DI Ronald was always appreciative of her honest endeavour, but now this is allied to her considerable initiative and drive. Generally there appears to be a lot of love in the air as Janet and Alice have also recently become engaged and a wedding date has been set.

As for DC Gordon, he is enjoying life and is revelling in his newfound romance. However, he and Jean Ronald were not content to have clandestine meetings after work, coupled with grabbing the odd loving look during work hours. They were well aware that for one to become romantically involved with one's direct line of command is frowned upon. Accordingly, Andrew agreed to a transfer and is now attached to a neighbouring police station. The end result is that they now live together and can be very open about their relationship and indeed their marriage plans.

Notwithstanding the reversal in the case against Miles Lamont, the career of Russell Holstein continues to go in an upward trajectory. His victories outnumber his defeats and he remains in big demand by instructing solicitors. In fact, Walter Bryson has instructed him on two or three occasions since the Lamont trial.

Joan Calvert continues to impress within the Crown Office and she is being handed more higher level cases. She and her husband, Jonathan, are expecting their first child. Given that IVF had failed for them, the fact that she has become pregnant is as much a surprise as it is a delight. Decisions still have to be made as to whether she will continue to work and Jonathan will be a house-husband or whether these roles will be reversed.

Andy and Carol Winters are now both incarcerated. Andy is in HMP Belmarsh while Carol is in HMP Bronzefield. They were both found guilty under Section 51 of the Criminal Justice and Public Order Act 1994 of having intimidated a juror. They were also charged with child abduction. They were each sentenced to six years imprisonment. They now communicate with each other by the occasional telephone call. Andy has still not fully forgiven Carol for revealing all to the police when questioned. Meanwhile, the police were never able to secure sufficient evidence to charge anyone in respect of the assault on Johnny Morgan. Nor were they able to persuade Andy and Carol Winters to give up the name of the person on whose behalf they were working. The natural assumption was that they had been instructed by Derek Lamont, but no direct evidence could be found in support of this.

Kenny Freeman, notwithstanding his name, is not in fact a free man. He, too, is an inmate of HMP Belmarsh. He was ultimately charged, convicted and sentenced to three years having plead guilty. Strangely he was very resigned to his fate and one almost gave the impression he was not actually opposed to going to prison. His life outside was fairly solitary and now at least he is able to enjoy the company of fellow inmates and not need to worry about where his next meal was coming from. Like Andy and Carol Winters, he too remained loyal to Walter Bryson and refused to advise the police who he was actually working for.

Michael Harding, the court officer, managed to escape a prison sentence due to his personal circumstances and the fact that he is a first offender. Also, true to her word, DI Ronald had made it known to the prosecution services that he had co-operated in their inquiries and assisted in securing other arrests. He was sentenced to six months community service. Of course, he was also immediately dismissed from his employment and the blot on his character may well provide issues for him when seeking re-employment.

Billy Blacker is still 'residing' at BMP Belmarsh but is no longer on remand having been found guilty of serious assault. He is in a different block from Miles Lamont this time around, but they have spotted one another from a distance.

Having served almost thirty years on the bench, Judge Oscar Templeton has retired, preferring to spend more time with his wife, children and grandchildren. It is also his intention to spend more time on the golf course.

Lara Watkins is totally in love with her little miniature dachshund, Oli, and everywhere that she does go, he is sure to follow. When she returns from school, Oli is always waiting at the garden gate to greet her.

And what of Mrs Edith Parker? Well, one year on and she is as nosey as ever!

THE END

About the Author

Brendan Maguire has three children, five grandchildren and two truly massive dogs. Brought up in Glasgow, latterly he lived by the sea in Troon, Ayrshire on the West Coast of Scotland. However, having fairly recently retired, he and his wife are most often to be found taking life relatively easy in the Orihuela Costa region of Spain.

Having secured a business degree, followed by a law degree (both at Strathclyde University) he then ventured into private legal practice and successfully ran his own business for many years. One of his areas of expertise was criminal law.

More recently, he decided to have a complete career change and opted for the travel industry. He set up a luxury tour operation, which ultimately employed 140 plus personnel.

Since retiring he has had time to engage in one of his favourite hobbies, namely writing. Some years previous he had a book published within the travel/humour genre. However, of late he has specialised in writing poems (mainly for children) and also short stories. In recent months he has won two writing competitions in the United States, one prose and one poetry. However one of his ambitions was always to write a crime novel - another tick on his bucket-list! On reflection, perhaps "Whatever it Takes" is therefore an apt title for his latest venture.

In addition to writing, Brendan would list his interests as playing golf, watching football, playing chess and dining out.

Printed in Great Britain
by Amazon

32674101R00169